*Western Fictioneers Presents:*

# WOLF CREEK: Hell on the Prairie

By Ford Fargo

James J. Griffin expresses his gratitude to Karl Rehn of
KR Training in Manheim, Texas, for his assistance with
information about weapons of the period.

Visit our website at www.westernfictioneers.com

Western Fictioneers

*Beneath the mask, **Ford Fargo** is not one but a posse of America's leading western authors who have pooled their talents to create a series of rip-snortin', old fashioned sagebrush sagas. Saddle up. Read 'em Cowboy! These are the legends of **Wolf Creek**.*

## THE WRITERS OF WOLF CREEK, AND THEIR CHARACTERS

Bill Crider - Cora Sloane, schoolmarm

Phil Dunlap - Rattlesnake Jake, bounty hunter

Wayne Dundee – Seamus O'Connor, deputy marshal

James J. Griffin - Bill Torrance, owner of the livery stable

Jerry Guin - Deputy Marshal Quint Croy

Douglas Hirt - Marcus Sublette, schoolteacher and headmaster

L. J. Martin - Angus "Spike" Sweeney, blacksmith

Matthew P. Mayo - Rupert "Rupe" Tingley, town drunk

Kerry Newcomb - James Reginald de Courcey, artist with a secret

Cheryl Pierson - Derrick McCain, farmer

Robert J. Randisi - Dave Benteen, gunsmith

James Reasoner - G.W. Satterlee, county sheriff

Frank Roderus - John Hix, barber

Troy D. Smith - Charley Blackfeather, scout; Sam Gardner, town marshal

Clay More - Logan Munro, town doctor

Chuck Tyrell - Billy Below, young cowboy; Sam Jones, gambler

Jackson Lowry - Wilson "Wil" Marsh, photographer

L. J. Washburn - Ira Breedlove, owner of the Wolf's Den Saloon

Matthew Pizzolato - Wesley Quaid, drifter

## THE WOLF CREEK SERIES:

Book 1   *Bloody Trail*
Book 2   *Kiowa Vengeance*
Book 3   *Murder in Dogleg City*
Book 4   *The Taylor County War*
Book 5   *Showdown at Demon's Drop*
Book 6   *Hell on the Prairie*
Book 7   *The Quick and the Dying*

*Appearing as Ford Fargo in this episode:*

HELL ON THE PRAIRIE............Troy D. Smith
DRAG RIDER..........................Chuck Tyrell
THE OATH.............................Clay More
IT TAKES A MAN....................Cheryl Pierson
ASA PEPPER'S PLACE..............Jerry Guin
MULESKINNERS: JUDGE NOT...Jacquie Rogers
NEW BEGINNINGS ...........……James J. Griffin

# INTRODUCTION

In Wolf Creek, everyone has a secret.

That includes our author, Ford Fargo—but we have decided to make his identity an *open* secret. Ford Fargo is the "house name" of Western Fictioneers—the only professional writers' organization devoted exclusively to the traditional western, and which includes many of the top names working in the genre today.

Wolf Creek is our playground.

It is a fictional town in 1871 Kansas. Each WF member participating in our project has created his or her own "main character," and each chapter in every volume of our series will be primarily written by a different writer, with their own townsperson serving as the principal point-of-view character for that chapter (or two, sometimes.) It will be sort of like a television series with a large ensemble cast; it will be like one of those Massive Multi-player Role-playing Games you can immerse yourself in online. And it is like nothing that has ever been done in the western genre before.

This particular volume is the first of our Wolf Creek books to be an anthology, rather than a collaborative novel- we'll do this from time to time in order to bring more depth to our characters.

You can explore our town and its citizens at our website if you wish:

http://wolfcreekkansas.yolasite.com/

Or you can simply turn this page, and step into the dusty streets of Wolf Creek.

Just be careful. It's a nice place to visit, but you wouldn't want to die there.


Troy D. Smith
President, Western Fictioneers
*Wolf Creek* series editor

## HELL ON THE PRAIRIE
### By
### Troy D. Smith

"*Hell on the Prairie!*" Marshal Sam Gardner slammed the newspaper onto his desk in disgust.

"Did you read this trash?" he asked his deputies.

Quint Croy shrugged. "I seen it, yeah. When that drummer coming in on the train from Wichita brought it in here, and said you might like to have it. I never picked it up and read it, though."

"How about you?" Sam asked the other deputy, Seamus O'Connor.

The huge Irishman shrugged as well. "I skimmed over it some."

Sam grunted. "Well, I guess you're too damn tall to read anything too close."

Sam and Quint were both puzzled over that comment, but their boss's comments often puzzled them, so they let it go.

"Listen to this," he said, picking the paper back up. " 'Sodom and Gomorrah would blush, we are told, at the vice and iniquity that run rampant in the southern end of Wolf Creek, the area that locals have given the appellation 'Dogleg City.' It is said that Negroes, Mexicans, and Celestials have the run of that neighborhood, making it into a heathen Empire where white Christian lives are as cheap as they were in Nero's Rome.' "

"Well, that's malarkey, right there," Seamus said. "We ain't even got that many Mexicans this time of year."

1

The marshal ignored him. "But this!" he thundered, jabbing the page with his forefinger. "This is what really chaps my hide. Listen!"

Quint stifled a yawn. He had the graveyard shift, which had ended two hours before, and was having trouble concentrating on anything other than his awaiting cot.

"'Nor is the so-called reputable part of town much better,'" Sam read aloud, "as corpses are stacking up like cordwood in the town square. Wolf Creek is developing a reputation as one of the most 'wide-open' towns on the frontier, its legacy being written in the blood of its hapless denizens. It has truly earned the sobriquet so aptly bestowed upon it –Hell on the Prairie.'"

"What does it mean by 'hatless denizens'?" Quint asked, his voice a little slurred by fatigue.

"Sobriquet is Mexican for hat, I think," Seamus said with a sly grin.

Sam spared them an annoyed glance, then continued.

"'Much of the blame for the town's unfettered lawlessness can be laid at the feet of the itinerant *pistolero* the town fathers have employed to organize Wolf Creek's constabulary, one Samuel Horace Gardner.'"

Seamus braced himself for the wave of fury that would surely be flowing from the marshal at that accusation. Quint yawned again.

"'Marshal Gardner,'" Sam continued, "'son of a prominent Illinois attorney who often crossed paths in the courtroom with Honest Abe Lincoln himself, by all accounts acquitted himself with considerable gallantry in the recent War of Rebellion.'"

Seamus brightened. "Here, now, Sam," he said. "That sounds nice enough."

"For what it's worth," Sam said. "Listen to what comes next."

Sam rattled the paper, then read on.

"'Tragically, Mssr. Gardner has squandered his great promise, and his noble bloodline, descending into a veritable maelstrom of immorality and vice; a profligate gambler with his lecherous fingers in sundry licentious pies, Gardner is widely considered to be a puffed, preening popinjay. Of late he has adopted the affectation of never being seen in public without a silver-headed cane, to draw attention and sympathy to a wound he received whilst failing to protect his town from a horde of leftover Secessionists.'"

"Mess yer Gardner?" Quint asked, puzzled.

"M'sieur," Seamus said, no longer wishing to toy with his exhausted comrade. "It's a fancy way of sayin' mister."

Quint shook his head. "There's an awful lot of foreign words in this newspaper. I don't understand half of what this jasper is sayin'."

"Well," Seamus replied, "it *is* a St. Louis paper, after all."

"What this jasper is saying," Sam declared, "is that every misdeed since Cain struck down Abel can be laid at my door, and I am unfit for my position."

"I'd like to see him try to keep a lid on this kettle," Quint said, indignant on his boss's behalf. "I doubt if there's a man alive who could do half as good a job as you do, Marshal."

3

"Hear, hear," Seamus said. "A hearty amen to that."

Sam sighed. "I appreciate your loyalty, boys. But if this keeps up, I may be out of a job."

"What are we gonna do about it?" Quint asked.

"Go over to the *Wolf Creek Expositor*," Sam said, "and fetch David Appleford over here, the grinning weasel."

Seamus was puzzled. "*The Expositor's* a local paper," he said. "Appleford has no hand in what's being printed in St. Louis."

"He has no direct hand," Sam said. "But the Wichita papers picked up on the foolishness he's been printing here in Wolf Creek, and now the St. Louis rags are picking it up from *them*. Before you know it the whole country will be printing this horseshit. Our town fathers are a herd of asses, but I don't think they want their city known as 'Hell on the Prairie'."

"I don't know," Seamus said. "I think it has sort of a ring to it, if you ask me."

"No one did. Just get Appleford in here. And wake up Quint and tell the poor boy to find a better place to snooze than my office chair."

A few minutes later, Seamus herded David Appleford through the door, a rough hand on his shoulder.

"Hello, Marshal," Appleford said, smiling uncomfortably. "Can I do something for you?"

Sam shoved the paper at him. "Read this."

Appleford bent over the desk. His smile broadened, and became sincere.

4

"Hell on the Prairie!" he said. "The St. Louis *Dispatch* has picked up my nickname for Dogleg City. Look, they even mention my name near the end, as a 'voice of civilization crying out in the wilderness'."

"You'll be crying out in the wilderness, all right," Sam said. "It's bad enough you make these wild claims here in town, now they're blowing around the damned countryside like tumbleweeds."

"Why, Marshal," Appleford said. "Sometimes your profanity verges on poetry."

"And sometimes," Seamus said, bending over the wiry editor, "my foot verges on your arse. It's vergin' right now, as a matter of fact."

Appleford did his best to ignore the large Irishman.

"Marshal," Appleford said. "Nothing sells newspapers quite as well as a truth no one else is willing to articulate."

Sam's right eyebrow arched. "By God, sir, you do have some brass," he said.

"Put yourself in my place," Appleford said. "Consider what has happened in the past few months. Children and schoolteachers shot and trampled in the street. The whole town barricaded up to defend against an attack by Kiowa Indians. An old-fashioned duel. Bounty hunters and gamblers shooting it out in saloons. A range war outside town. More schoolchildren shot. An old lady gets her brains blown all over the front door of the Methodist Church, and the preacher's wife gets kidnapped right from under your deputy's nose. If that's not going to hell, I'd sure like to know how you'd have me describe it."

5

Sam grimaced. "I don't deny," he said, "we've been having an active spell. But criticizing this office doesn't make things any better. It just contributes to more disrespect and more disregard for the law."

"I report the news, marshal, and I call it like I see it."

Sam nodded thoughtfully. "There's a lot to be said for that," he said at length. "I call it like I see it, too. Fact is, some things have come to my attention lately. One or two little secrets about our esteemed newspaperman that I'm sure the good folks of Wolf Creek would find quite newsworthy. My biggest decision would be which one to start with."

Appleford blanched.

"Are you –are you threatening me, Marshal?"

Sam grinned, "Why, I'm not sure, old hoss. Depends on whether you think your little secrets are threatening or not."

They were interrupted by the front door slamming open. Mason Wright, the baker, rushed through it, red-cheeked and breathless.

"Marshal Gardner!" he exclaimed. "Thank God you're here!"

"Hello, Mason," Sam said. "I don't recall ordering any pies, but I'm never averse to one."

"I ain't here about pies, Marshal! There's a fella in front of the Lucky Break says he's looking for you. Says if you don't come quick he's gonna go inside and start shootin' whoever strikes his fancy."

"That's odd," Sam said. "On a normal day, there'd be a good five or six men at the Lucky Break who'd shoot

6

anybody who threatened to break up one of their card games."

"This fella says his name is Lane Downing," Mason said.

"That explains it, I guess," Sam said. "No one wants to get on his bad side."

"Lane Downing?" Seamus asked.

"I forget you haven't been out west long, Seamus," Sam said.

"Lane Downing," Appleford explained, "is one of the most famous gunslingers in the west. He's left a trail of corpses in his wake from here to San Francisco. They say his speed with that Colt of his is unnatural."

"I suppose I'd better go see what he wants," Sam said, standing up.

"I'll get the shotgun," Seamus said.

"No need for that," Sam said. "I can handle him."

David Appleford gasped audibly. "Marshal!" he said. "You can't be serious –you need to get a posse together. You can't go out there alone!"

"Well, Mr. Appleford –not to be impolite, but he didn't invite *everybody*, just me."

Appleford wasn't convinced. "Look, you don't have to do this to prove anything, because of what I've been writing. No one would expect you to do that. Any sensible man would take reinforcements to face Lane Downing."

Sam took his hat from the rack. "I'll be back directly, Seamus. And Mason –you have set my mind on pies, can you run fetch me one of those rhubarbs?"

"Um, yes sir, marshal," the baker said.

Sam passed through the open door. He did not take his cane.

While walking westward toward the Lucky Break, he was joined by Samuel Jones, that establishment's house gambler and an accomplished gunfighter in his own right.

"Hello, Marshal," Jones said.

"Hello there, other Sam," the marshal replied. "What brings you out this time of day?"

"I was just on my way to work, and someone told me Lane Downing is causing a ruckus over at the Lucky Break. I thought maybe you could use an extra gun."

"That's real decent of you, Samuel," the marshal said. "But you just go on to work, I don't need an army to deal with one malcontent."

Jones nodded knowingly. "I'll stay close by, just in case," he said.

"Whatever suits you."

Suddenly, Sam Gardner stopped in his tracks. He slowly looked back over his shoulder.

Seamus was following him at a discreet distance, lugging the shotgun. David Appleford walked beside the deputy, notepad in hand. Seamus tipped his hat at his boss.

"I feel like I'm leading a wagon train," the marshal said.

He finished the trek to the Lucky Break. Jones dropped back, to walk beside the deputy and the newspaperman.

There was no mistaking Lane Downing. He stood in the middle of the street, smiling wickedly from under a broad sombrero.

"I hear you were looking for me," Sam Gardner said.

"You heard right," Downing responded. "I wasn't sure you'd show up."

"I don't think we've had the pleasure."

"You're right again," Downing said. "But you met Galan Hagney, up in Denver, a couple of years back. You shot him dead, in fact."

"Seems like I shot several people up in Denver, a couple of years back, I didn't bother keeping them straight. What was this one to you?"

"Well, to be honest, Marshal, I never met him, neither. But his brother's a friend of mine, and I offered to even the score for him."

Briefly –only for an instant, really –Downing's eyes flickered to the crowd of onlookers who stood in front of the saloon. One of them quickly glanced back – both he and the man beside him were strangers to town, and both were keeping their hands suspiciously close to their holstered pistols.

Sam smiled. Lane Downing felt the need for reinforcements, just in case. He wasn't as cocky as he sounded.

"Downing," Sam called out, "I have a pie on its way to my office, and you're wasting my time. I assume this is all about your desire to have a new dead lawman to put on your credentials. I'm standing right here, you're not going to get it done by talking to me."

For the next two or three seconds, time slowed down for Samuel Horace Gardner. It was always thus. His mind emptied itself, his gun became an extension of his body. All his attention was focused on his target, and other potential targets, and everything else disappeared. This had first happened in the early days of the war, in the heat of battle. It was like playing a game of chess, all the way through, in one's own head, before ever the first move was made. It was fast as lightning, slow as thunder, sure as death.

And it was the only thing in life Samuel Gardner had ever truly been good at.

He gloried in it. He was in absolute and complete control, in a way he never was during the so-called peaceful pursuits of life. Those, for him, were only filler for moments like this, when he was *alive*. It ultimately didn't even matter whether he lived or died, won or lost, those potential outcomes were not even wisps of thought for him. He only *was*.

Three shots rang out from Sam's pistol, in such rapid succession some onlookers thought it had been only one. Lane Downing, in all likelihood, never had time to realize his life was over –one instant he was making his move, grasping the butt of his Colt, and the next he lay dead in the dust. His two partners, too, died with their guns half-drawn. One of them twitched a couple of times after he hit the ground.

Sam stood for a moment, arm extended, smoke curling from his barrel. Then he holstered his weapon and turned around.

Seamus had not had time to lower his shotgun. Jones stood with his gun in hand, but had not fired it. Appleford had dropped his notepad in the street, and stood with mouth agape.

The crowd of onlookers was silent, awed as well. Sam had been hired on the force of his reputation, but had rarely been forced to display his talents so openly. Some of them had secretly begun to doubt the stories about him. They doubted no longer.

"Other Sam," he called out to Jones. "Are you going straight to the gaming tables, or do you have time to stop by my office and sample that pie with us? Young Quint put a fresh pot of coffee on before he passed out. We have a piece for you, too, Appleford, if you promise to stop standing there slack-jawed."

"Yes –yes sir, Marshal," Appleford said. The four of them walked back toward the office together.

"And if I might add, Marshal," Appleford said, "I believe you'll be more pleased by the story in our next edition."

"Yes," Sam said, smiling, "yes, Mr. Appleford, I dare say I will be."

Wil Marsh had already appeared, as if from thin air, and set up his camera –he was taking photographs of the corpses before the marshal was out of sight.

THE END

DRAG RIDER
By
Chuck Tyrell

*Texas, 1868*

1

Billy's Pa never came back from the war. They never got word that he was dead, but more than three years after Appomattox, he'd not showed up, and Billy made up his mind. He just had to tell his ma. Hat in hand, he clomped into the pole-and-mud cabin that served as the Gladstone home.

"Go wash your hands and face, young man," Elva Gladstone said. "No son of mine is going to eat with dirty hands."

"Didn't come to eat, Ma," Billy said.

"Then what?"

Billy held his hand out.

"Gold? William Henry Gladstone, have you robbed someone? Are you a bandit?"

"No'm. But I sold twenty-five steers to Walt Brodrick. Four bucks a head. So I could bring you a hunnert in gold."

"Twenty-five?"

"Yes'm. I been watching them mavericks in the brush and catching me a calf ever now and again to cut 'n

12

brand. Took purt near two years to get twenny-five with a G-slash brand on 'em."

"Did you steal cattle, William?"

"No'm. Mavericks's free fer the taking. Get 'em outta the brush. Brand 'em. Then drive 'em north."

Elva Gladstone stood silent for a moment. Then she held out her hand. "Thank you, William. The money will hold us until father returns."

Billy emptied the five double eagles into his mother's outstretched palm. "Pa ain't coming home, Ma. 'N me, I'm going to Kansas with Walt Brodrick."

"You are what?"

"Going to Kansas."

Elva Gladstone's mouth opened, then closed, then opened again. She tried to speak, but no words came. Tears filled her eyes. She swiped at them with the back of her hand. "Gets dusty in here," she said.

"Walt's gonna have horses for me to ride, and he's paying me twenty-five dollars a month, and that's just starting pay. He said that if I ever made top drover, I'd get twice that much."

"Kansas?"

"Yup. To the railhead. Walt told me a man named McElroy'd set up a shipping operation at a place called Wolf Creek, and Walt's gonna take a couple a thousand head of cows up there." Billy couldn't keep the smile from his face. Cattle made money, and ranchers needed cowboys to tend those cattle. May even come the day when Billy Gladstone would be a rancher himself.

"Besides," he continued, "Timmy's twelve –he's big enough to do the chores around here."

13

Elva squared her shoulders and stiffened her back. "We'll make out," she said. "I'd better get something together for you to take along."

"One a' Walt's riders's coming by in the morning with a remuda horse for me."

Elva nodded and turned away. "Go wash your hands and face," she said.

"Yes'm." Billy spun about and ran for the pitcher of water and washbasin on the stand by the pole-and-mud cabin's back door.

\*\*\*

"Hello the house!"

The sky had just begun to lighten in the east when Walt Brodrick's rider hailed the Gladstone place. Billy and Timmy had already been up for more than an hour, and smoke from Elva Gladstone's cooking fire rose from the laid rock chimney.

"Hello the house!" The holler came again, before anyone could answer the first one.

Elva opened the front door. "Don't be impatient, young man," she said. "Breakfast will soon be ready, if you don't mind biscuits and bacon with a little milk. Your name, please."

"I reckon I'll be Landerson Willis," the young cowboy said. "Folks call me Reckon. Where's Billy?"

"Milking the cow, not that she's giving much. No bull to hand to give her a calf."

"Biscuits 'n bacon'd do good, missus, real good, I reckon."

"Get down. Tie your horses over there to the scrub oak, where there's grass." She turned toward the door,

14

then stopped. Looking back over her shoulder, she said, "Water and a wash basin outback. Wash your hands and face before you come in to eat."

Reckon had already kneed his pony toward the clump of oak, but he reined up. "You talk just like my own ma," he said, grinning. "I'll surely wash up, ma'am, I surely will, I reckon."

"See that you do."

Reckon tied the horses to the scrub oak as directed, then strode to the back side of the cabin. Two boys already splashed in the washbasin, trying to outdo each other as to who could get the wettest. "Which one a' you is Billy?"

"Me," Billy said.

Reckon looked him over. The boy lacked two inches or so of Reckon's height, but his shoulders were broad, and muscles rippled on his arms as he completed washing up.

Billy wiped his face with a scrap of flour sacking. "This here's my brother Timmy," he said.

"I'm Reckon. Come to getcha. Yore pony's tied to the scrub oaks out front."

"We leaving right now?"

"Yore Ma gave me an invite to biscuits 'n bacon, I reckon. We can ride after that. If'n you can ride that pony, that is."

"If'n that pony wears hair, I c'n ride 'im."

"I reckon," Reckon said, but he didn't sound convinced. "Outta the way. Let a man wash up."

"Bet my Ma told you to do that."

"So?"

Billy grinned. "She would, I reckon," he said.

15

"Yeah. I reckon," Reckon said as he splashed water into the basin.

"See ya inside."

Billy and Timmy charged through the door, shouting something about breakfast, but when Reckon entered, they sat respectfully on one side of the table.

"You sit over there," Elva said, waving at a bench on the side opposite Billy and Timmy. She placed a platter heaped high with biscuits on the table, to complement the bacon that sent a delicious smell wafting around the kitchen.

Reckon looked at Timmy and Billy, expecting them to dive into the food.

"If you'll remove your hat, Mr. Willis, we'll say grace." Elva folded her arms.

Reckon grabbed his hat and put it in his lap. "Sorry," he mumbled.

"Timmy, say grace, please."

"Yes'm."

Silence.

"Timmy."

"God, thank you for the grub. Bless it for us. Amen."

Elva heaved a sigh. "Someday you'll learn to be humble," she said, "someday."

Billy, Timmy, and Reckon Willis sat poised to strike, looking expectantly at Elva for permission to delve in.

"You may eat," she said, and they reached for the food. While they ate, Elva sat with her hands in her lap.

"Mighty fine feed," Reckon said after he'd swallowed his last mouthful of bacon and biscuit. "Mighty fine, I reckon."

"Why thank you, Reckon Willis. That's kindly of you to say so."

Reckon stood. "Be the same with you, ma'am, me and Billy'd best hightail it for Hawley Flats. Boss's gathering the herd there."

Billy gathered up his plate and cup and took them to the stand at the back wall. "I'll be going," he said.

"God keep you, William," Elva said. She hadn't moved since the men started eating.

"Thankee for the grub, Missus," Reckon said. "Right tasty first thing in the morning, I reckon."

"You're welcome, Reckon Willis. And I'll trust you to keep an eye on William. He's not been away from home for any amount of time."

"Yes'm," Reckon said. "Let's light a shuck, Billy Boy. Boss'll be upset at us taking so long."

"I'm ready," Billy said.

"You think," said Reckon. "You still ain't forked that feisty little bronc I brung for you to ride."

"I will. I will." Billy clamped a floppy felt hat on his head. "Let's do it," he said.

Out by the scrub oaks, Billy got his first good look at the Texas pony Reckon had brought for him. "Where'd you dig this one up?" he said.

"He's been around a couple a' year. A bit feisty, so cowboys ain't happy to have to ride him."

"Got a name?"

"Pick any cuss word. It'll fit."

17

Billy put a hand on the pony's scrawny neck. "Looks like he ain't been eating too regular."

"That there blaze-faced hunk a Hell could spend a month knee-deep in clover and never gain a ounce. He was born skinny. He'll die skinny, I reckon."

The horse twitched an ear and slapped Billy's leg with a long uncut tail. "Hang on, horse, I'll be right back." He dashed around the house toward the root cellar.

Reckon sat his bay horse with a leg thrown over the saddle horn. He rolled a smoke as he watched.

Billy came running back.

"We ain't got all day," Reckon said. "You gonna fork that bronc or not?"

"Climb on a horse what don't know ya, and you're likely to be eating dirt, least that's what my Pa always said. And you all said it'd be a wonder if I could ride this horse here. Well, me and him're gonna get acquainted." Billy held out a shriveled carrot so the paint could have a sniff.

The horse's head came around to where he could nibble at the carrot. "You see, paint horse, I ain't of the bad sort," Billy said. "They ain't no reason for you to get a hump in your back before I even get a leg across it."

The paint horse butted Billy, looking for more carrot.

"Not now, horse," he said. "But you be good to me and I'll be good to you. Deal?"

"I reckon it's getting high time to move out," Reckon said.

"Sometimes it takes longer when a man's in a rush," Billy said. "That's what my Pa said anyway. Up,"

18

he said to the paint as he tugged on the horse's onside front leg. The paint let Billy pick up his forefoot without a fuss, and stood patiently as he used his Barlow knife to clean the frog and check the shoe.

"He'll need re-shoeing a long time before we get to Kansas," Billy said. He went around and lifted the other forefoot. "Rock jammed into the frog," he said. "Don't you all take care of your horses?"

"I reckon the wrangler does," Reckon said.

"Don't look like it." Billy checked the paint's rear hooves, trimming where it was needed. "See, old man? You look after me. I'll look after you."

"Shee-it," Reckon said. "Trail horses don't get no pampering."

"Maybe not. But a man looks after his horse and the horse'll look after him." Billy untied the paint and fastened his warbag to the saddle. "We'll get a proper saddle at the rail head," he said. "Gotta leave mine here for my little brother." He fed a second carrot to the paint. "What do you figure? You gonna sunfish a bit before we settle down?" He patted the paint, then led him around in three tight circles. He ran his hand around under the horse's belly, then took the surcingle up another notch. "We ready to go, paint?"

"William Henry! Are you leaving with no goodbye for your mother?"

"I'll be on my way, Ma." Billy didn't turn to look at his mother as he spoke. He raised his voice. "Timmy. You listening?"

"Yeah." Timmy Gladstone stood at the corner of the cabin.

"You're all Ma's got, boy. I'll go make some cash money. You keep the place together, you hear? You're already twelve, so stand up and bear it."

"You ain't my Pa," Timmy said, "and you got no right to go telling me what to do." The pout on his face was plain in his voice.

Billy's tone took on a hard edge. "Pa gets home and you can go back to being a little boy. Right now you're the man on this place. Act like it."

"I reckon we'd better get going," Reckon Willis said.

"Be right with you," Billy said. But as he shoved his left boot into the stirrup, a hump came up in the scrawny paint's back. Billy barely got his right leg over the cantle when the paint leaped straight up and came down on four stiff legs to give Billy a spine-jolting before he sunfished around in a tight circle, doing his damnedest to dislodge the rider from the saddle.

Reckon Willis let out a holler. "Whee-ooh. Ride 'im, you all. Whee-ooh. Yeehaw."

Billy hauled on the reins, trying to get the paint's head up from between his legs. It wouldn't come, and the paint wasn't about to stop sunfishing.

The daylight between Billy's butt and the saddle got wider and wider until he was coming down when the paint was going up and the smack of buttocks on saddle seat sounded loud and clear, and Billy rebounded high and far, his boots came clear of the stirrups, and he found himself in a heap on the ground.

The paint stopped the moment Billy hit dirt.

"Ain't no way to ride a hoss," Reckon said.

20

"That paint don't know me, that's all," Billy said. He rubbed his backside with both hands. "You figure it's just me? Or does that horse buck everyone off?" He limped over to where his hat lay in the dust, picked it up, and used it slap the same dust from his clothes. The paint stood hipshot, its head hanging.

But the moment Billy took the reins again, the horse's head came up and he turned it to give Billy a sniff. "It's me, old pard, and I'm bound to ride you to the herd. Either that, or die."

One moment Billy was sweet-talking the paint, the next he was in the saddle with the reins pulled tight, holding the paint's head up.

The horse crow-hopped a bit. Then he decided Billy had the upper hand. He settled down and let his head droop.

"There. See? Not such a bad situation," Billy said. "Now. We've got a couple dozen steers to haze over to Hawley Flats. Let's get to it."

The paint never tried to throw Billy again, and it turned out to be the best trail horse of his entire string, despite its coloring.

## 2

The Brodrick herd started north from Hawley Flats with Billy Gladstone riding drag along with Hillary Mason, a rider who'd seen many better days and some days a lot worse, to hear him tell. Hill Mason was pushing fifty if he was a year, and he said he fought with Hi Morgan in Terrell's Cavalry at Mansfield and Yellow

Bayou. But whenever Billy asked about the fighting, Ol'
Hill would give him a hard eye and shake his head.

"You don't want to hear about war, boy," he'd say.
"There ain't no heroes and it ain't fun. War is as close to
Hell as a man can get. Leave it be."

At Red River Station, the day before the Brodrick
herd crossed the river into the Indian Nations, a man drove
into camp in a rattley old wagon. He talked to Brodrick
and to L.B. Higgins, the trail boss. Then he parked the
rickety old wagon across the main fire from the Old
Woman's chuckwagon. And when Billy came in for
supper, the man had rows of guns laid out on a ground
cloth.

"Yer pick a' weapons, men," the man hollered.
"Injun Nations comin' up and a man orter be ready. No
tellin' what them redskins's gonna do."

Billy tried hard to ignore the gun hawk. The
Gladstones only had one squirrel rifle, and Billy left it at
home for Timmy to help fill the dinner pot with. He
wandered over to the firearms display with a plate of beef
and beans and a hunk of sourdough.

"Well, youngster. Innerest you all in a reliable
weepon?"

"Just looking," Billy said. He had no money, and
drovers got paid after the herd reached railhead and got
sold.

The gun hawk wore a patch over one eye and he
only had three fingers on his left hand. "You'll be wanting
a lead spitter in the Nations," he said. "Man cain't depend
on no one but his own self when the cards is down."

22

"Get the Remington conversion, kid," Walt Brodrick said.

"Ain't got no money, boss."

"How much for the Remington, Hoss?"

"Fer you, Walt, one eagle'll do. One lousy eagle."

"Good buy, Billy," Brodrick said. "Man needs a good six-gun on the trail. Rifle, too, if he can."

"Ain't got no money, boss," Billy said again.

"You got wages coming at railhead, boy. I'll foot you the Remington and take it from your pay."

Billy reached for the Remington.

"Model 1858 Army," said the gun hawk. "Been converted to .46 rimfire. Damn good piece." He picked up the Remington and held it out, butt first, to Billy. "Box a' fifty cartridges comes with the gun."

"Sweet deal," Brodrick said.

Billy took the big Remington. Its weight felt reassuring in his hand. He looked at Brodrick. "Think I should, boss?"

"Better deal than a three-day drunk," Brodrick said. "Cowboys spend their pay on rotgut whiskey at trail end anyway. You all'd be that much better off with the Remington and bullets. But it's your call."

Billy nodded. "I'll do it if this here gun man can be trusted. Boss, you say he got these pieces legal-like and they'll not blow up in my face when I pull the trigger?"

"You can trust Hoss, boy," Brodrick said.

"Done," Billy said. He thrust the Remington behind his waistband and held his hand out. "Bullets," he said.

23

The old man fished around in his wagon and came up with a box of shells for the Remington. He gave them to Billy. "Ten bucks, Brodrick," he said.

"Later," Brodrick said. "You know I'm good for it."

While the man Brodrick called Hoss tried to sell guns to other cowboys, Billy took his food and the bullets back toward the chuckwagon. "Gonna use the tailgate for a minute," he told the Old Woman, and set the box of bullets down while he wolfed the beans and beef and sourdough bread.

"Taking my cookin' space awful generous, aincha?" The Old Woman shifted his chaw and spat a stream of tobacco juice to one side.

Billy finished chewing and swallowed. "Mighty fine grub," he said.

"Shee-it. Y'all'd josh an old man to death."

"Got me a gun," Billy said. "Bought and paid for. Well, almost paid for anyways." He put the plate down and pulled the Remington out. "See?"

The Old Woman touched the Remington with a gnarled forefinger. "Model 1858," he said. "Allus did like a Remington gun. They's built to last 'til the cows come home."

Billy used the edge of his neckerchief to wipe a bit of dust off the barrel. "Not bad, I'd say. Not bad."

"I got a piece of good leather," the Old Woman said. "Reckon a man could make a purty fair holster with it."

"Ain't got no money, Old Woman."

24

"You got strong arms and a good back, though. You get me firewood when you ain't riding drag, and I'll give you the leather and let you use my awl, too."

"Done," Billy said. Working for stuff was nothing new to him. He scraped the last of the beans off his plate and into his mouth, popped the last hunk of sourdough in with the beans and started chewing.

The Old Woman rummaged around in the chuckwagon's storage cupboards and came up with a rough-cut piece of leather so old it was the color of chewing tobacco. "Looks like shit," he said, "but its still good leather." He snapped the leather a couple of times to rid it of dust, then wiped it on the seat of his pants.

***

Billy turned fifteen the day Brodrick's herd swam Red River out of Texas and into the Indian Nations.

Brodrick crossed the river first, riding a big black horse and testing the depth of the water and footing on the bottom. "Roll 'em," he hollered as the black humped up and out of the river back on the Texas side.

"Heeyah. Come on. Git on there!" Shouts came from all sides, and lariats whacked against the cowboys' legs as they pushed the reluctant cattle into the river. The chuckwagon took the ferry across back at Red River Station, east from where the herd crossed.

By the time Billy and the other drag rider reached the riverbank, the herd stretched from Texas to the Nations. More than two thousand head of longhorns pushed through the muddy Red. The lead steers clambered out of the river on the far side about the time the drag riders pushed the stragglers into the water on the Texas

25

side. For a moment Billy pulled paint to a stop and watched the herd make its way across, a great undulating beasty looking thing that broke up into individual steers as the beeves reached firm ground at the northern bank.

"Heeyah. Heeyah." Billy slapped a lagging steer on the rump with his coiled lariat. The reluctant animal jumped at the slap and suddenly found itself in the water. Other steers moved north, so the laggard did, too.

Reckon Willis came back along the line of cattle from his swing rider position. He hollered to Billy. "Only gotta swim a couple a hunnert feet. If your paint gits to having trouble, slip off and just hang on. If'n he gets ahead of you, grab aholt of his tail. Got it?"

"I'll make it, Reckon," Billy hollered back. He just wished he was as confident as he thought he sounded. Still, even as the tail end of the herd moved away from the Texas bank, Billy sat paint, glued to the spot. There was a lot of water in the river, more water than Billy had ever seen. At home, there'd not been enough water in one place to learn to swim, and now he had to swim paint, and maybe himself, across Red River. A tremor ran through his body.

"Hey!"

Billy's eyes focused on Reckon Willis, who beckoned him with a swinging arm.

"Getchor cracker ass across the goldam river," Reckon hollered.

Billy took a deep breath. He chucked paint with his heels and the horse obediently stepped into the water, following the cows he'd been tailing for so many miles. Billy just hung on.

Twenty-five or thirty yards out, the water was up to paint's belly, him standing no more than fourteen hands or so.

The Old Woman told Billy to leave his boots and his Remington in the chuckwagon when he carried an armful of firewood over before breakfast. "Water's hard on iron and leather," the Old Woman said. You leave them things here." Billy did as he was told, and now, with water coming up around his thighs, he was glad he did.

Long before paint reached the north bank, he was neck deep in the muddy water of Red River. The little horse kept his nose above water and his hind feet on the bottom in the deepest parts. Billy slid out of the saddle and let the paint tow him as he kept a hand on the saddle horn. When he could tell the horse had all four legs on the river bottom, he pulled himself back into the saddle.

Once in the water, the steers seemed interested only in following the press of cattle ahead of them, so drag riders could do the same. Still, Billy heaved a sigh of relief as paint humped himself up onto the sand flat leading to the north bank.

"Hustle them dogies along." The shout came from Reckon Willis. "Boss says there's a good flat to bed down on about three miles north. Yeehaw! We're outta Texas, bound for Kansas, and they ain't nobody ta git in our way!"

Billy doffed his hat and waved it at Reckon to show he'd heard. "Come on, paint," he said. "We got work to do."

The cattle trailed water so the miasma of dust that defined the world of the drag rider didn't materialize until Red River was out of sight behind them.

Brodrick never pushed his cattle more than about ten miles a day. Any faster and the steers ended up at the railhead little more than skin and bones. Ten to a dozen miles gave the herd time to graze before bedding down. "Keeps meat on them bones," Brodrick said.

Billy had enough time to scavenge a couple of armloads of wood for the Old Woman before Brodrick called him over. "You got the midnight watch," he said, "you and Mitch."

"Gotcha," Billy said. He dumped the wood and dug out the leather from the chuckwagon cupboard. He measured it against the Remington and used his Barlow knife to cut the leather to shape. He had a leather thong in his warbag, and he used that to lace the soon-to-be holster together. He'd left a long shank on the back side so he could put slits in it, fit the laced holster through, and have a natural place for his belt to go.

After dark, drovers who weren't on night duty gathered at the fire. Brodrick didn't allow drinking on a drive. "Cows 'n booze don't mix," he said. That meant yarning after dark and drinking cup after cup of Arbuckle's coffee.

"'Member that gal Rose down to San Antone," said Long Tom. Billy'd heard his name was Justin Thomas, but everyone called him Long Tom because he had the longest peeder anyone ever saw. Second cousin to Brodrick's stallion, they said. "I remember her oh-so-well. Rose got her name 'cause she always patted herself down with rose water before . . . well, before."

"Before what?" chorused half a dozen drovers. They knew the story.

"Well, just before. Made a man just wanna get plumb nekkid before he got down to business."

"Plumb?" one of the younger drovers asked, wide-eyed. His name was Alfred Duncan, but for some reason everybody called him Sonny.

"Plumb, stick-stark nekkid. An' you know what? Rose'd take a washcloth and a basin of water and wash all the trail dust offa ya. Ever' bit, ever'where."

"Gol," Sonny said, fingering his crotch.

"Gol is right," Long Tom said. "Ain't nothing like rolling around in a bed of roses with a purty gal who smells like roses all over, and I *do* mean all over."

"You sniffed her everywhere?"

"Son, they ain't much about Lilac Rose that this ol' son don't know. Once I get to San Antone, she's the onliest gal I see."

Billy didn't say anything, but he purely wondered what it would be like to be with a woman *that* way. He picked up his saddle blanket and saddle and lugged them over to the remuda. Lorenzo Gomez wrangled for Brodrick, and the boss wouldn't stand for any ragging on Lorenzo because of his Mexicanness. "Best man I ever seen with cayuses," Brodrick said. "Don't want any of you be coming down on Lorenzo because he looks Mexican. His folks's been in Texas longer'n any of us. Treat'im with respect, dammit."

"*Noches,*" Lorenzo said.

29

"Need to catch the roan," Billy said. "Midnight watch tonight, n' she's the best night horse in my string."

"Go get him, Billy Boy. He waits patiently, I think."

"*Gracias*," Billy said, shaking out a loop in his lariat. He stepped into the rope corral that kept the remuda from straying, and tossed the loop over the head of the roan he called Berry.

The roan followed meekly, good-natured horse that she was, even though Lorenzo called her "he." Billy had picked a soft-looking place to sleep, and –as all drovers did –he tied Berry to a peg he'd driven into the ground before he bedded down. When he didn't have night duty, he put down the saddle blanket to sleep on and covered up with his slicker, but the night was clear and the weather balmy, so Billy just curled up on the ground and went to sleep, using his arm for a pillow. The Remington lay in its new holster, near at hand.

While Billy slept, his right hand lying next to Berry's peg, six men on big powerful horses approached the herd from the wooded hills to the west. The herd's night riders, who crossed paths north and south as they circled the bedded cattle, were out of sight. The dark riders spread until they were fifteen to twenty feet apart. Each carried a heavy saddle blanket in one hand. Occasionally starlight would glance from the riders' eyes, giving them a peculiarly sinister appearance.

"Ready." The order came almost too quietly to be heard. The riders shook out the blankets and held them to the herd side of their horses with both hands.

"Now!"

As one, the riders popped the blankets and hollered. In an instant, the herd was on its feet and running.

3

The thunder of more than two thousand cattle on the run could not be mistaken for any other sound. The rumble of running hooves no sooner reached Billy's body than he threw off the slicker, grabbed the Remington and jumped to his feet, pulled Berry's reins free, and leaped aboard. On the run, he laced his belt through the Remington's holster and let it hang naturally. "Move it, Berry babe." Billy slapped the mare on the rump with his hat and he took out after the spooked cattle like a scared coyote.

Walt Brodrick came alongside, his black stallion easily keeping pace with Berry. "Along the river, kid," he hollered. "Keep 'em headed north."

"Right-o," Billy hollered back. Brodrick twicked the black's reins, and horse and rider disappeared into the dust cloud that followed the stampeding steers.

Berry and Billy headed down the south side of the stampede at a dead run. Even a small Texas horse like Berry was much faster than a longhorn steer. Billy began to gain on the cattle. He pulled his lariat from its ties on the saddle fork.

Reckon Willis came up beside Billy, the brim of his hat pushed back against the crown by the wind. "Gotta turn 'em," he shouted. "Push 'em west! Make 'em turn to the west!" He grabbed his hat from his head and slapped it against his horse's rump. It jumped ahead with a burst of speed.

There seemed to be riders ahead. Billy squinted, trying to see through the cloud of dust that hung over the herd. Big men, they were, on big horses. They rode in a line, cutting through the front end of the stampede.

"Hey! Them's B Bar beeves!" The shout came from Reckon Willis. The answer was a volley of gunfire. Reckon's horse went down.

Billy wasted precious seconds reattaching his lariat to the saddle fork. Then he drew the Remington that hung from his belt in its homemade holster. He eared the hammer back and looked for someone to shoot.

A dark shape showed. Billy assumed none of the Brodrick drovers would be so far east. He pushed the big six-shooter out at arm's length and held low, figuring it would be easier to hit a horse than the man riding it. He pulled the trigger. Exploding powder sent the .46 caliber bullet slashing through the dust.

The dark horse reared. Billy heard a whinny. He grimaced. Shooting horses was not what he signed on to do. He cocked the Remington again, aimed at the same animal, and pulled the trigger. This time, the horse went down.

Billy reined Berry wide of the downed horse, hoping to avoid the rider. He couldn't see Reckon anywhere, so he started pushing the lead steers, the ones left from the cutting action of the big men and their big horses. He left the Remington on half-cock and shoved it back into its new holster.

There was no rain and no lightning, nothing to keep the half-wild longhorns running. They began to slow. Billy rode at the head, slapping steers with his lariat and turning them west. Then Brodrick was there, and Sam Morgan, the kid called Sonny, and Long Tom. The herd turned and started milling.

"Good job, Billy," Brodrick said. "Don't look like we lost a lot of stock."

"I shot a horse," Billy said.

"A what?"

"A horse."

"Why in heaven's name would you go and shoot a horse?"

"Easier to hit than the rider."

"Rider?"

"Five or six. Big men on big horses. Cut off a bunch of our cows. I shot one of their horses. They shot before me, and Reckon Willis's horse went down, too."

"Show me."

Billy reined Berry around and rode back toward Red River. The big horse had gone down maybe half a mile behind, but there was no moon and the stars gave precious little light. Billy squinted, searching for a black lump that could be the downed horse, but it was Berry that led them straight to the dead animal. One minute Billy could see nothing, the next, a dark mound appeared ahead. He could soon tell it was a horse, lying flat on its side with its neck stretched out like it was still running full speed.

"Right here, boss."

Brodrick came up. He looked at the downed horse for a long moment, then swung his right leg over the cantle to dismount.

On the ground, he dug a Lucifer from his vest pocket and struck it alight with a thick thumbnail. He held the flickering flame over the hindquarters, then the dead horse's shoulder. "No brand on this side," he muttered. "Ain't often a cayuse is branded on the off side. Hmmm."

"There was half a dozen riders, boss," Billy said. "They cut out some beeves. They was on big horses like that one there."

"Hmmm." Brodrick remounted.

"Reckon Willis's horse went down, too," Billy said. "Them riders was shooting at us."

"No rider here. Got away, or off far enough so we can't see 'im. Let's go look for Reckon," Brodrick said. "Lead out."

Again, Billy let Berry pick the way back to where bullets from the big men had downed Reckon's horse. And again, Billy couldn't make out the shape of the downed pony until Berry stopped.

There was no lump in the darkness. Instead, dim whitish lattice of bare ribs showed. The dead horse had been trampled flat on the hard ground. Only its ribcage stood proud.

"Here," Billy said. "What's left of the horse is here." He searched the heavily trodden ground for signs that said Reckon had been trampled like the horse. "Don't seem that Reckon got trampled," he said.

"Hey!" a faint cry came from off toward the river. "Hey! It's me, I reckon."

Billy and Brodrick turned to stare into the darkness.

"Hang on. I'll be there directly." But he didn't show.

Billy still peered into the black night, searching for some sign of Reckon Willis, but all he saw was nothing. Berry sidled around until she faced the way Reckon's voice came from.

"Take him back to the chuckwagon," Brodrick said. "We'll come back for the saddle and stuff after daybreak." He reined the stallion around and spurred him away toward the herd.

"Billy? Billy? That you, kid?"

"I'm here, Reckon."

"Cain't walk. Could ya come over?"

"Yep," Billy said. He chucked Berry toward the sound of Reckon's voice.

"Watch out, man. Don't let that clumsy cayuse of yours step on me."

"Reckon!" Billy could see Reckon now, a darker shadow on the dark ground. "Can't you git up?"

"Nope."

"Jayzus," Billy muttered. He dismounted and dropped the reins on the ground. Berry knew not to stray when she was ground-tied.

Reckon Willis lay on his side with his knees drawn up. "Glad to see ya, kid. Almost figured I was done in."

"What's hurting?"

"Purty much ever'thing."

"Reckon you can ride?"

"Get me into the saddle. I'll ride," Reckon said.

35

Billy had seen men carry other men. He'd never tried it himself. "Give me a hand," he said.

Reckon Willis lifted an arm. Billy took hold of his wrist and squatted so he could bring the arm across his shoulders. "You're gonna have to do your part," he said. "I'm gonna try to stand up. You come alongside."

"Go to it."

Billy worked to straighten his legs, heaving Reckon to his feet as he rose.

"*Aaaargh!* Be gentle, kid!"

"Ain't no gentle way to do it, man, unless you want to wait for daylight so I can get some of the boys to help."

"Just making conversation."

"Hmmph. I'm going on up," Billy said, and again put all his muscle power into getting Reckon Willis to his feet.

Reckon moaned and screeched, but every time Billy acted like he was going to give up, Reckon would tell him to keep at it.

Billy finally got Reckon all the way over to Berry, to where he could hold the horn with his good left hand. "You get a good grip, Reckon. I'll put a shoulder under your butt and see if we can't get you up onto this here Berry mare."

Reckon said nothing, which Billy took for assent. He squatted and put a shoulder under Reckon's buttocks.

"Thanks for the horse, cowboys. Little cracker ass that she is."

*Shit.*

Billy froze, crouched, with his shoulder under Reckon's butt and no way to reach for his Remington.

36

Then he slid out from under Reckon so he could see over the saddle.

A big shadow came up on Berry's off side; a man dressed all in black, a man with charcoal or something rubbed on his face, a man who stood over six feet tall, if an inch, with thick shoulders that stretched the fabric of his shirt. Up close, Billy could see all that.

"Horse stealing and rustling'll getchu hung, mister," Billy said. "'Sides, my *compañero's* hurt, thanks to a bunch of rustlers."

"You're awful small to be talking so big. I'll take the cracker-ass mare."

Reckon Willis said nothing. In fact, he went almost completely limp, like he'd drawn his last breath.

"Weren't rustling cows," the big man said. "Just exacting a toll, that's what. Just a toll for passing through here." He pulled Berry's head around, but she planted her feet wide and stubborn and refused to move.

"Come on, cayuse," the man said.

But with Reckon hanging onto the horn, Berry knew her rider wasn't seated right and she wouldn't budge.

"Stupid damn hoss," the man said.

Billy wondered why the man hadn't pulled a gun. Lost when the big horse went down?

"I'm gonna let you down," he said to Reckon and stepped away. But Reckon still hung onto the horn with his good hand.

The big man jerked Berry's head around and yanked on the reins. Stubborn to the core, Berry stood with her legs spread wide and her head down.

"Damn mare," the big man said. "Turn yourself around."

Billy stood in Reckon's shadow and worked the Remington out of its tight new holster. The click made when he carefully eared the hammer back was next to inaudible. The gun had only three live rounds in it because he'd forgotten to reload after taking those shots at the big man's big horse. At the very least, he figured, the big man trying to steal Berry was one of the outfit that ran off B-Bar beeves.

Just as the big man got ready to give Berry's reins another jerk, Billy put the Remington across the saddle seat and pointed it right at the big man's chest. "Mister, I don't like the way you're treating my little mare. Berry's sensitive. Now this here Remington's loaded and cocked, mister, and if I can hit your horse at fifty yards, I sure as Hell can hit you from across this saddle."

The big man's hands stopped sudden-like. He held them about shoulder high, forearms at right angles with his upper arms. "Now, boy. No need for misunderstandings here."

Billy could see him coiling up, it seemed, like a rattler getting ready to strike. With snakes, you killed 'em before they could kill you. He pulled the trigger.

The .46 caliber chunk of lead took the rustler in the hollow of his neck, punching a hole through his windpipe and his esophagus, then shattering his spine as it tried to exit.

The big man dropped without a sound. Berry stood still, like the good night horse she was.

"Get 'im?" Reckon's question was a hoarse whisper.

"Yeah." Billy's hands shook as he belatedly shucked empty shells from the Remington and refilled its cylinder.

"Get me on the goldam horse," Reckon said. "Cain't hold on much longer."

Putting shoulder to butt and straining upward took the shakes from Billy's body, but he didn't really want to look at the big man who lay dead, sprawled where he'd fallen.

Clawing and straining by Reckon, and pushing and shoving by Billy, finally got Reckon up into the saddle. "You'd better have a look at that thing there on the ground," Reckon said. "Might be something useful on 'im."

"Ain't never killed nobody before," Billy said. Even his voice shook.

"Him 'er us. That's what it was, I reckon."

Light started to show in the east. The land tuned from dark gray and black to stretches of brownish gray land and stands of greenish black loblollies and water oak.

"You sitting on that saddle good?" Billy asked.

"I reckon."

Berry stood still, ignoring the dead man on the ground next to her.

"I'll have a look at the rustler, then." Billy stepped gingerly around his mare and peered down on the big man. The growing dawn made it a lot easier to see, and Billy bit his lip at what he saw. The dead man's eyes were wide open, like someone had really surprised him, but they were dry, not shiny at all. His face was untouched, but the entry hole in his throat was now a pool of blood, and his neck crooked at an odd angle.

The raggedy growth of whiskers on the rustler's face said he'd been out of town for some time, but it wasn't thick enough or long enough to brand him as a mountain man. And his black clothes weren't worn enough or dirty enough to say he was a long way from home. Billy dug his fingers into a shirt pocket that showed a bulge. He came up with a bag of shredded tobacco and a little pipe that looked carved of hickory. The other shirt pocket held nothing. The big man's holster was empty. Somewhere, he'd lost his six-gun. Maybe when his horse went down.

Billy grabbed an arm and turned him over. No rear pockets on the California pants, so he turned him back. Front pockets yielded a couple of half-dimes and a Barlow knife. A big splotch of wetness said the rustler had peed his pants, and the smell that hit Billy as he searched the man's britches pockets said he'd shat himself, too. Billy wrinkled his nose as he unbuckled the big man's gunbelt and pulled it free.

"Nothing much," Billy said. "I'll give it to the boss."

"Yeah. Let's do it," Reckon said. But when Billy reached for Berry's reins, the rumble of galloping horses came from the west, and Walt Brodrick and three drovers rode over the rise in a cloud of dust.

"Never mind, boss's here," Billy said.

Brodrick's stallion came to a stiff-legged hopping stop next to the dead rustler. "Whatta we got here?"

"I reckon he was riding that horse I shot," Billy said. "He tried to steal Berry, so I shot him."

Brodrick stared at the rustler, who stared at the sky. "I'll be damned," he said.

"He had this stuff," Billy said, holding the tobacco, pipe, Barlow knife, and half-dimes out to Brodrick. The gunbelt hung over Billy's shoulder.

"Did, eh? Well, you just hang onto them things."

Chill Craven, one of the drovers, sidled his horse over to where he could see the big man's face. "I know that rannie," he said. "Know him to see him, anyways. That's Orville Hicks, little brother to Melvin Hicks. Some say you get on the wrong side of one of them Hicks, you gotta deal with them all."

"He come thieving my cows," Brodrick said. "He got some of what he deserved." He reined his stallion around. "Leave him lie," he said. "And Craven, you come with me. We'll go have a look at the horse Billy shot. The rest of you help Billy and Reckon get back to the chuckwagon. The herd's quiet. Soon as I get back, we'll move 'em five or six miles north." Brodrick and Craven rode off, leaving Reckon and Billy with one horse, flanked by Jerry MacGuire on one side and Terrel Davis on the other. The Old Woman had hot coffee on when they got to the chuckwagon, but then, if the wagon wasn't moving, the coffee pot was always hot.

Billy put Berry back with the remuda, where he caught and saddled another of his string, a lineback dun he called Wellan, and rode out to help with the herd. The Old Woman would take care of Reckon, but the cows needed someone to look after them. That's what drovers were for.

Broderick came back to camp with a saddle and blanket, a Henry rifle and scabbard, and a Shawk and McClanahan percussion pistol, .36 caliber. "We'll keep the saddle, Billy," he said. "You want this Henry? Got a decent saddle scabbard. Never hurts to have a long gun, and this one uses the same cartridge as your short gun."

Billy picked up the Henry. It was a heavy gun for a 15-year-old, but it felt good in his hands. "You gonna just give this here Henry rifle to me, boss?"

"You earned it," Brodrick said. "And from now on, you ride swing east of the herd, you hear?"

"I hear you, boss." Billy couldn't help but smile. He was out of the dust cloud the herd raised when it moved. Well, almost out.

Brodrick let out a holler. "Get to it. We gotta get this herd to Wolf Creek."

4

Brodrick paid the Cherokees a dime a head so they'd let the herd pass through the Indian Nations. He never tried to track down the beeves cut out by the Hicks gang. "Be more trouble than it's worth," he said. "Bound to be gun play if we catch up to them, and it's more important to get these beeves to Wolf Creek anyways."

Reckon Willis was back to driving the herd by the time they reached Wolf Creek, not far into Kansas.

The Old Woman parked the chuckwagon next to a stand of box elders. Billy gathered firewood, as he'd promised back when the Old Woman gave him the leather for a holster. It wasn't a fancy one, but it kept his converted Remington Army in easy reach, and he'd had a little time to practice with the six-gun. Nothing special, and Billy had no intention of becoming a pistoleer, but he'd use the Remington if he had to, like he'd used it at Red River.

Billy released the paint into the remuda. For once, he didn't have a night watch. He went and stood on the bank of Wolf Creek. On the far side, there was hardly anything to see. Holding corrals. A couple of tents. A frame building of some kind.

When Billy got back to the chuckwagon, a stranger stood talking to Brodrick. He was a straight-standing man. Maybe a soldier, or someone who'd been a soldier. After Billy got a plate of beef and beans from the Old Woman, he sidled over close enough to hear what the man was saying.

"Walt, I tell you. This is gonna be the closest place to load beeves for Chicago. There'll be a railhead here early next year. Kirt Evans –he's a railroad man –told me."

"I hear you, McElroy. But I got cows here right now. Cain't hold them here for a year or whatever."

"Look. I told you I'd buy your beeves, and I will. Like I said, I'll give you forty bucks a head. I just can't give all of it to you at once."

"So how much are we talking about?" Brodrick didn't look pleased at McElroy's statement. He stooped, plucked a long stem of foxtail, and started chewing at the end.

"Twenty bucks now. Twenty more when you come with another herd next year."

"Shit."

"Not a bad deal, I'd say. What'd you pay for the beeves? Four dollars? Five? Even if I welched on the second twenty, which I won't, you'd make a good return on your herd."

"Shit."

"Walter Brodrick. How long have you known me?"

"Since West Point."

"Have I ever lied to you?"

"No."

"I'm not going to start now, either. Even if you did wear gray and me blue."

Brodrick tossed the chewed foxtail stem away. With his head bowed, he kicked at a clod and sent it skittering out into the dark. He heaved a sigh. "I'll do it, McElroy, just because it's you."

"Good," McElroy said. He shoved out a firm hand.

Brodrick shook it. "We'll start moving the beeves across Wolf Creek in the morning."

"Put them in the holding pens," McElroy said.

"You got it," Brodrick said. "Have your counters ready. The steers'll be there before noon."

"Good enough. I'll be waiting." McElroy tossed the dregs in his tin coffee cup into the fire. "Good cuppa, Sullivan," he said. He tossed the cup in the dishpan and saluted Brodrick. "Walter," he said.

"Daniel," Brodrick said, giving him the same salute.

McElroy mounted a big dappled sorrel and splashed across the creek.

"Sullivan?" Billy laughed. "Sullivan? That McElroy man called you Sullivan."

44

"Mind yer own business," the Old Woman said.

Billy chuckled. Every chuckwagon cook was the Old Woman. "I'll never call you by that name," he said. He put his tin plate in the dishpan and went to look for a soft place to bed down.

To Billy, it seemed he'd no more than closed his eyes than the Old Woman was beating on a pan and hollering for everybody to get up and eat or he'd toss breakfast into Wolf Creek. Billy had his bay horse saddled and ready, so all he had to do was grab a couple of biscuits, pull them apart, add three slices of bacon each, and climb aboard.

Taking bites of biscuit and bacon, Billy steered the bay remuda horse out and around the grazing herd, two thousand head and some, spread out and cropping at buffalo grass, covered a pretty big chunk of territory. Billy had not yet reached his eastern swing position when he heard Brodrick's deep voice ring out.

"Roll 'em. Roll 'em. Get these lazy critters across Wolf Creek. We ain't got all morning. Roll 'em!"

Billy shoved the last hunk of biscuit and bacon into his mouth, loosed the leather strap that held his lariat, and gathered the hard rope into his chapped and callused hands. He slapped the lariat against his chaps. "Heeyah. Heeyah!"

The nearest steers moved away from the bay, but immediately went back to cropping buffalo grass. Billy kneed the bay around, keeping him pushing the steers north toward the Wolf Creek crossing.

Dust began to rise.

Months up the trail first opened by Jesse Chisholm, and there had been no rain to speak of. Lucky. No rain means no lightning to scare the spooky longhorns into a stampede. Besides the little run started by the Hicks gang back at the Red, Brodricks' herd hadn't stampeded even once. Despite walking nearly a thousand miles all told, the longhorns didn't have the gaunt look of a hustled herd. They had meat on their bones. McElroy was getting a good herd.

"Heeyah. Heeyah." Billy slapped his coiled lariat at a laggard steer. The big longhorn turned his head and gave the bay horse the bad eye. Billy slapped him again. "Move on there, you brainless hunk of meat. Heeyah. Heeyah."

The steer decided picking up his pace was the better part of valor. He lifted his tail and trotted off, leaving splotches of manure in his wake.

Billy chuckled. They'd been trailing the herd so long that they knew every steer by sight and hand tagged many with disrespectful names. The one that had just splotched the grazing ground with green shit was exactly that –Shitface, and he'd be Shitface until the day he went under the butcher's knife. Billy wondered for a moment if the steer's meat would carry the fetid aroma of his manure. "Heeyah. Heeyah." He slapped Shitface again.

The first steers waded into Wolf Creek crossing. The stream ran fast, but was no more than ten inches to a foot deep, and the bottom was gravel rather than shifty sand like that of the Red River crossing.

About an hour after the lead steer stepped into Wolf Creek, Billy reined his remuda bay into the crossing as well. The steers walked readily across, as there was nothing to eat in the creek and lush grass beckoned on the far side.

The bay stopped and took a long drink of creek water. "That's a good boy," Billy said. "Drink up. The water's free."

"Heeyah. Heeyah." Drag riders pushed the last of the herd into the creek as Billy's bay humped up the far bank.

"We're gonna hafta cut 'em up," Brodrick shouted. "Four holding pens. A quarter of the herd in each pen. Roll 'em out!"

He rode up to Billy. "You ride through, Billy. Cut the herd in half. Move."

Billy turned his bay horse into the herd. He used his lariat on the longhorns coming up on him, tapping them on the forehead and making them flinch back and turn inward. The drag riders had stopped pushing at the rear end of the herd, so those Billy turned back milled into a compact mass. They stopped and went to cropping at the buffalo grass.

On the far side of the herd, Billy turned back. He and the bay pushed the forward half of the longhorns toward the holding pens. Two had gates open, so it wasn't hard work to haze about five hundred steers into each.

McElroy's men straddled the pole corral fences, counting longhorns as they came through the gates.

"Five oh three," one shouted.

"Five sixteen," hollered another.

"All right," Brodrick said to the drovers. "Let's get the rest of 'em."

47

In all, Brodrick's herd counted out at two thousand and thirty-two head of Texas longhorns. All twenty-five of the steers he'd bought from Billy were among them.

Daniel McElroy's operation was housed in a place with plank walls and a canvas roof. That's where Brodrick paid his drovers. As he was youngest, Billy came last. Brodrick sat at a long wooden table with benches on each side. "Billy, I figure you at a month riding drag and nigh on to two months on swing. I put your pay at ninety-five dollars and I'll round that out to an even one hundred, because of the grit you showed at Red River. You can keep the Henry and two of the horses in your remuda string. That good with you?"

Billy stammered. "Sh . . . sh . . . sure." He had no idea swing riders got more than drag riders.

Brodrick put four gold eagles on the table, then an eagle, a half eagle, and some folding money. "You take care, son. People here know you cowboys got paid, and they're gonna try their level best to get that money from you, and they don't care a lick about being fair about it."

"Yessir."

While he was outside getting Paint, his first choice from the remuda, Billy took a minute to make sure no one was looking. He pulled the Henry, shoved the four gold eagles into the end of the saddle scabbard, and put the rifle back.

The frame building turned out to have a saloon on the ground floor and rooms on the upper. There was even a bath out back, shielded by canvas.

The first place B Bar riders went was the frame building. Most went straight for the saloon. Billy and

Reckon, who still had a limp, opted for a bath, even though they had no clean clothes to change into. After that they went to the saloon. The sign said it was the Lucky Break. "Hey, Reckon. You ever been in a saloon?" Billy asked.

"Hell, yes. Um. Well, I looked in the door to one."

"Shee-it."

"All the B Bar hands is in there, I reckon. Let's go get in on the fun."

Only ten B Bar cowboys in the saloon, but they made enough noise for twice their number and more. Two were bucking the tiger at the roulette wheel. Three were in a game of cards at one of the tables. Three scattered along the bar with women by their sides. Women!

Billy remembered what Long Tom said about the girl in San Antone, the one called Rose. He looked again, and sure enough, Long Tom stood at the bar with a woman pressing up against him.

Reckon bellied up to the bar like a seasoned drinker, even though it was no more than a plank laid across three barrels. Billy stood next to him.

"What'll it be?" a man asked from behind the bar.

Billy looked at Reckon. "Couple of whiskeys, I reckon," Reckon said.

"Good thing," the man said. "Whiskey's all we got." He used a dipper to get whiskey from an open barrel and put two fingers worth in two glasses. "A buck fer the two," he said.

Reckon paid him with paper. "You get the next round," he said to Billy, "bottoms up."

49

Reckon opened his mouth wide, tossed the contents of the glass inside, and swallowed. Tears came to his eyes and he coughed against the back of his hand. "Not bad," he said when he was able to speak again. "Not bad."

He eyed Billy and waved at the whiskey glass on the bar. "Cowboys down it all at once. First time anyway. Makes drinking go easier after that. 'Sides, I bought that sumbitch for ya."

Billy tossed the whiskey, and swallowed. It burned. It burned in his throat and it burned in his gullet. He had no doubt but that it would burn his anus when it came out that end. Then the pain went away and the fire banked into a warmth that gradually spread through his body.

"Not bad," he said, his voice still strained from the impact of the raw whiskey on his vocal chords. "My turn. 'Nother round of whiskey for me 'n my friend."

The man behind the bar ladled two fingers of whiskey into the glasses. "Be a buck," he said.

This time Billy hunted through the paper money he'd been paid with. He found a dollar bill and passed it to the barman.

Reckon tossed his drink.

Billy tossed his drink.

The two cowboys looked at each other squinty eyed, tears leaking. They nodded. "Not bad," they chorused.

The warm glow spread and everything Billy looked at took on a rosey hue. "Rose," he said.

"Huh?" Reckon faced the room and hooked his elbows on the bar.

"Buy a drink for a lady?"

The question came at Billy's elbow. He glanced sideways at the woman, then did a double take. "Rose?" he said.

"Lily," she said. "But I'll answer to Rose if you want."

"Lady wants a drink," Billy said. His lips were warm and numb, and his words slurred a little.

The barman filled a glass with something brown. It didn't look like whiskey, but Billy didn't care. "Four bits," the barman said.

Billy gave him another dollar bill.

"I'll hold on to the change. She'll be wanting another when that one's gone," the barman said.

Billy nodded. *Good man, that barman.* But then, at that moment, the whole world looked good to Billy.

"Let's go sit," Lily said. "One empty table over there." She nodded at a table in a corner behind the stairway at the far end of the room.

"Sure, Rose," Billy said.

Lily took his hand and led him to the table. He managed to hold onto his whiskey glass and she held her glass of brown liquid as if she'd done it many times before.

"Hey, kid." Long Tom lurched over to the table. "Hang on ta that gal 'til I win me some money bucking the tiger, then I'll be along." He guffawed at his own joke and staggered away toward the roulette table.

Lily leaned over to whisper in Billy's ear. "I don't want to be here when that oaf comes back. I've got a room upstairs. Wanna come?"

Billy stared at Lily. She looked rosy to him. He couldn't see the thick powder nor the extra lip rouge. He didn't notice the rubbery roll around her hips, nor the crow's feet wrinkles in the corners of her eyes. She just looked rosy. "I think I'll have another drink," he said.

"I got booze in the room," she said. "You can pay me. Cheaper than paying Jigger for everything."

"Jigger?"

"The barman."

"Oh. All right, then."

Lily nearly leaped to her feet. She grabbed Billy by the hand and almost dragged him to the stairway. Billy wagged his head, trying to spot Reckon, but couldn't. Then they were at the top of the stairs. "Just down the hall," Lily said in a low voice. She led him to a room with the name LILY over the door. She gave Billy a smile as he watched her pull a key from her bodice. "Nobody looks there, hardly," she said. "Good place to keep what a gal don't want others to find." She opened the door. "Come on in," she said. Billy did, and Lily locked the door behind them.

"Ain't no place to sit but the bed," Lily said.

"You said you got whiskey up here. You said that."

"Sit down," Lily said. She grabbed him by the hand, twirled him around, and gave him a little push. The edge of the bed caught him behind the knees and he had to sit down. "There. That's better." She plucked his hat from his head and sailed it across the room. It landed on a steamer trunk. She sniffed Billy's hair. "Hmmm. A bath, eh?"

"Didn't have no other clothes, though," Billy said. "Whiskey?"

"Good Lord. Don't you think of nothing but drink?"

Billy ducked his head. "Do," he said.

"Do what?"

"Do think of other things."

"Like what?"

"Rose."

"That your sweetheart?"

"Nah. Long Tom's."

"No! What're you doing thinking nasty things about someone else's girl?"

Billy kept his head down. "He tol' us. He tol' us everthing what him and Rose did. Makes a man think."

Lily plonked herself down by Billy. "What? Tell me what."

"Cain't. Cain't say stuff like that to a woman."

"Have anything to do with this?" Lily patted the tent in Billy's trousers.

All he could say was "ung."

Lily laughed. "Maybe we could do some of those things."

Billy's face went bright red. "Ah. Ah. Ah," he said.

"No. No. No. Can't be." Lily laughed again. "Youngster, how old are you, anyway?"

"Sixteen, next birthday."

"Man growed, then." Lily started unbuttoning Billy's shirt. "Just you leave it all to me, Billy Boy. Everything's gonna be just fine. You shut your eyes and lay back and leave it all to me."

Billy did what he was told.

In the morning light, Billy could see all the wrinkles and bulges that Lily had, but he didn't care. "Gotta get back to the herd," he said. He put an eagle on the commode. "This enough?"

"More than enough, Billy Below."

"Whaddaya mean, Billy Below?"

"I'll always know how you like it, Billy Below."

Billy grinned as he left the Lucky Break. Billy Below. A good name for a droving cowboy.

When Billy signed on with Tobias Breedlove at the T-Bar-B to help watch after the herd through the winter, that's how he signed his name.

Billy Below.


THE END

## THE OATH
by
Clay More

When he first entered the spartanly furnished room, Doctor Logan Munro had thought that the baby was about to die. Its breathing was harsh, rasping, and the cough was pitiful to hear.

The air was thick with the acrid smell of tobacco. As soon as his eyes accustomed themselves to the pall of smoke that made the dim circle of light thrown out from an oil-lamp even dimmer, he began to assess the situation.

"He's here with my ma," chirped up Tommy Brewster, the seven-year-old boy who had been sent to summon him.

His stepfather was a large red-faced man with a full beard, whom Logan recognized as Rob Parker –the chief bartender at The Lucky Break Saloon. He was sprawled over the bed, resting his head on a bank of pillows. He had a half-empty bottle of whiskey in one hand, and a smoldering cigarette in the other. He squinted belligerently at Logan.

"You took you-sh time, Munro," he slurred. "My kid is sick and…"

Logan ignored him and crossed to the distraught and frightened mother, who was rocking back and forth as she tried to placate the badly distressed baby.

"Please, Doctor Munro, help him," she pleaded. "He can't breathe."

"You besht give him medicine quick, Munro," the drunken bartender said, swinging his legs off the bed and rising unsteadily to his feet.

Logan turned to him and jabbed the man's chest with his forefinger. "You are a disgrace, sir. You are both drunk and disrespectful. You will address me as Doctor Munro in the future." He grabbed the cigarette stub and tossed it into the open front of the Pot Belly stove that was blazing away nearby. "For now," he said, "take yourself out of this sick room, get rid of that whiskey, and do not dare come back in with a cigarette."

"You better not talk…"

"Get out now, Rob Parker, before I manhandle you out. You are wasting precious time."

"Please, Rob, the baby," Mollie Parker begged. "Just go and let the doctor look at little Kenny."

Rob Parker lumbered out.

"Tommy, open that window and let some clean air in, please," Logan said. He doffed his hat and bent to examine the baby.

"How long has he been breathing as bad as this, Mollie?"

"About four hours. He'd been stuffed up all day, but this evening he started to burn up, and the cough just got worse and worse. From around midnight, his cough has sometimes sounded like a puppy dog barking."

"Hold him firm while I have a look down his throat," he said. He reached into his bag, moving aside the Beaumont-Adams revolver that he always kept there, to bring out a tongue depressor and a small mirror. He angled the mirror so that he could reflect some light from the lamp into the baby's mouth, while he eased the tongue down to see the throat.

There were two things he hoped not to see. First was a purulent web-like membrane that was typical of diphtheria. That would be really bad news, because an epidemic could spread like wildfire through a town like Wolf Creek. The immediate danger with such a discovery was that it could instantly block off the baby's airway and choke him to death.

The second thing was a cherry red protuberance down the back of the throat if the epiglottis was inflamed. The trouble in that case was that it was so easy to send the larynx into spasm to shut down the whole of the throat, again with catastrophic results. If either was present, Logan was ready to perform an immediate tracheostomy, by making an incision in the baby's throat between the Adam's apple and the cricoid cartilage just below it. He kept a small wooden case with a fresh scalpel and a silver tube for just such an emergency in his black bag.

But fortunately, there was no evidence of either. He withdrew the tongue depressor.

"Is…is it the diphtheria, Doctor? My sister died from it when I was about Tommy's age."

Logan drew out his stethoscope and fitted the earpieces into his ears. "No, Mollie. It isn't diphtheria, it's just a bad case of croup." He listened to the infant's chest for a few moments then looked up and nodded. "We can settle him down nice and easy." He turned to young Tommy. "Close that window again, son, then go and call your father in. I need him to stoke that stove and fetch as much water as possible in your kettle and in a couple of pans."

As the youngster went off with the message, Logan explained. "The linings of his upper air passages are inflamed, raw, and bulging. They need steam to reduce them. We need to fill up the room with steam, and you'll see him settle before your very eyes."

***

It took an hour for young Kenny Parker's breathing to calm down, and another hour for the cough to subside enough to satisfy Logan that he could safely leave the child for a while.

By that time, Rob Parker had sobered up some.

"I'm sorry, Doctor Munro," he said, somewhat sheepishly. "I guess I was worried about our little boy. When I get nervous I reach for the bottle." He scratched his beard. "And I have to admit that I probably had a couple too many last night at The Lucky Break. Dab Henry was in a celebrating mood about something that he didn't want to tell us about. That usually means he's clinched some sort of business deal."

Logan shrugged dismissively. He was aware of Mayor Dab Henry's varied business activities. He didn't consider them to be any of his concern.

"Just don't smoke near your son for a few days," he said.

"We can't thank you enough, Dr Munro," Mollie said, placing a hand on his arm as he snapped his bag closed and prepared to leave.

"My pleasure, Mollie. I have to admit that I was relieved to find that it wasn't diphtheria myself."

58

It was close to seven o'clock by the time he left their clapboard house on the east of town that looked directly out on the Wolf Creek River itself, and made his way back to his office and home at the corner of Second Street and Washington Street. It was too late to go back to bed, but too early to stop at Ma's Café to sample one of Stephanie Adam's fine breakfasts. Accordingly, he let himself into his office and sat down at his roll-top desk, where he had left the notes that he was preparing for his monograph on Venereal Diseases. After almost twenty years spent practicing medicine and surgery, his body was used to doing with less sleep than most people.

He charged his meerschaum pipe from the tobacco jar on top of his desk and struck a light to it. When it was going to his satisfaction, he shuffled through his papers and then set to write the section on syphilitic chancres, the painless ulcers that formed on the genitals at the start of the condition. There had certainly been no shortage of cases in Wolf Creek over the time that he had practiced there, and at one time he had thought that it would be good to publish his monograph complete with photographic plates of them. He had toyed with asking some of his less particular patients if they would mind their private parts being captured for the benefit of science. Against that was the fact that he would have to hire the services of Wil Marsh, the Wolf Creek photographer. He personally doubted that the man could be trusted not to keep copies and exploit them in some way. Marsh struck Logan as being the sort of chap who would dig up and sell his grandmother's coffin if he could make money from it.

He was roused from his writing about forty minutes later, when his pipe had long gone out and the ashes had gone cold, by a rapping on his consulting room door. He glanced at the wall clock and sighed. It was not even eight o'clock, more than an hour before his consulting time on a Tuesday, so whoever it was clearly felt that they needed urgent medical attention.

"OK, I'm coming," he called as the knocking continued.

He opened the door to behold a dapper man of about his own age, dressed in a fancy suit with a low-crowned hat. In his hand was a silver-topped Malacca walking stick, which accounted for the loudness of the rapping. He had a thick but well trimmed goatee beard, black tie and black gloves. His face was pale and he looked in pain. A thin patina of perspiration covered his brow.

"Ah, Doctor Logan Munro, I presume," he said, glancing sideways towards the sign that hung by the doorframe. "Please accept my apologies for my lamentable timing, sir. It is just that my damned leg is killing me."

He brought the cane down hard and thwacked his left leg with it. There was the loud smacking sound of wood on wood, but he didn't as much as wince at the contact.

Logan looked down and saw one elegant, highly polished boot. Beside it was a wooden peg leg that started just below his knee.

"It hurts like hell, doctor. I would deem it a great service if you could help me out."

60

Logan looked up at his face and saw a startled look flash across his it, as if a sudden pain had pierced through him. Then his eyes fluttered, and he swayed for a moment before collapsing forward into Logan Munro's arms.

***

After carrying the man to his couch, Logan gave him a volatile waft of spirit of sal smelling salts to bring him round, before helping him sit forward enough to take a mouthful of medicinal brandy.

The man swallowed, then stared at him for a moment, his expression one of bemusement.

Logan smiled reassuringly. "You fainted, sir. Nothing more."

"Excuse me again, Doctor Munro," he said with a wan smile. "The name is Barclay Patterson. I just arrived in Wolf Creek yesterday and I found to my horror that I have left my medication at my last hotel. I usually take my first dose as soon as I get up, and without it I am in agony."

"Where is the pain, Mr. Patterson?"

"This is where you will think me mad, Dr. Munro. It is my wooden leg, it feels cold and it has a shooting pain, as if I am being stabbed by cold steel all the way down."

"Do you mean the stump is paining you?"

"No, sir. It feels like it is my own leg as it was before it was cut off. I get this feeling all the time, even when I am not wearing this damned peg leg. I can feel the pain in my toes, even though I know they are not there."

"And can you wriggle these invisible toes?"

61

"I feel as though I can. It sort of makes me feel as if I am mad."

"You are not mad, Mr. Patterson. I've come across it a lot since the War and figured out that it happens when certain nerves were not adequately separated, and they end up getting inflamed. The brain then messes up the signals from the nerves and it thinks it is feeling pain."

Barclay Patterson wiped some perspiration from his brow and gave a wan smile. "That's a relief to know – that I'm not mad."

Logan crossed the room and picked up a magazine from a pile in the corner. "This is the latest issue of *Lippincott's Magazine of Popular Literature and Science*," he explained as he thumbed through it and returned with it folded open at a page. "Curiously, here is an article by Dr. Silas Mitchell of Philadelphia. He started up a 'Stump Clinic' back there the year after the War ended. He calls them 'Phantom limbs.'"

Barclay Patterson ran his eye over the page, then, to Logan's surprise, tossed his head back and laughed. "So I'm not mad," he said after he stopped laughing. "I'm just haunted. Haunted by my own goddamned leg!"

\*\*\*

After administering a dose of laudanum mixed with valerian, a combination of his own invention, Logan brewed coffee and sat talking with Barclay Patterson. He knew from experience not to pry too much into where and when a man lost a limb. Some volunteered it freely, others were far more reticent, which was understandable considering that feelings about the War still ran high and those who had lost limbs had maybe more than most to be resentful about. All that Barclay Patterson would let out was that he had fought for the Union and felt let down by the benefactions that the government had announced for those who had lost limbs during the war.

"Benefactions! Hogwash! They talked about us all getting new limbs!" Barclay exclaimed sourly, before giving a short sarcastic laugh. "And what did I get? Just this damned piece of timber that hurts so much."

He took a sip of his coffee and then pointed with the cup at the wall above Logan's desk, at his framed degree, a framed copy of the Hippocratic Oath, beside his citation for the Crimean and Turkish Medals from the Crimean War, and to the picture of Helen and himself on their wedding day in Lucknow, surrounded by his comrades from the British East India Company.

"You seem to have travelled a lot, doctor. And I see that you are married. Does your good lady like the frontier here?"

"I am a widower," Logan returned, his eyes threatening to well up at the thought of Helen. "She died in India."

"My condolences, Doctor. I am a widower also. The hurt never goes, but I found that it softens." He pointed to the framed oath, screwed his eyes up to read, then recited:

"'I swear by Apollo, the healer, by Asclepias, Hygieia and Panacea and by all the gods and goddesses of the pantheon...'" He smiled. "Mighty fancy words. I am guessing this is the famous Hippocratic Oath."

"It is, Mr. Patterson. Like all university-trained doctors, I took that oath the day I qualified. I find it a good philosophy for life."

He stood up and crossed to his medical bag. He delved inside and drew out a small bottle. "Here is enough laudanum to keep you going for a couple of days. Come back then, and I'll have a fresh supply ready for you."

Barclay Patterson lay his coffee cup down. "That's a big bag you have to carry around, Dr. Munro. I suppose you need to carry a lot of medicines and instruments about with you?"

"I have to be prepared for any eventuality, whether it is to deliver a baby, set a broken bone or dig out a bullet. Wolf Creek may look like a sleepy frontier town, but all sorts of things happen here."

"I imagine so."

Barclay Patterson paid the bill, replaced his wallet, then leaned forward and pushed himself upright –with surprising nimbleness –and held out his hand.

"Seems to me the good folk of Wolf Creek are lucky to have you, Dr. Munro. I'll call back as you ordered for more of this life-saving medicine. And now, I wonder if I could trouble you a little more. I am partial to the odd hand of poker. Are there any establishments that could accommodate me here in Wolf Creek?"

"Saloons and gaming houses we have in plenty, Mr. Patterson. All supplied with their own professional gamblers. I would caution you to be careful, sir." He told him where each of them was to be found.

When he had left, Logan wondered whether Barclay Patterson was an honest gambler or not. If not, then he would have a real need to be very careful indeed.

\*\*\*

Logan was kept pretty busy over the next week with an outbreak of dysentery that seemed to rattle its way through Dogleg City and then filter across Grant Street. He had seen twenty-three cases, and prescribed his own concoction of tea made from slippery elm bark, sweet gum, willow and dogwood to each one. Between visiting these emergencies and keeping his regular consulting hours, he had scant time to eat or sleep, let alone check up on some of his regular patients. Among those that he had managed to re-visit were some of the folks that had been wounded during the Kiowa raid on the town a few weeks before, and little Kenny Parker. Fortunately, the baby had not had a recurrence of the croup attack.

Mollie Parker was apologetic about her husband's drunkenness and his behavior.

"Rob is a good man, but when he takes too many whiskeys at the saloon he doesn't know when to stop. But he is a good father to Tommy and Kenny. He worries about them."

Logan had listened sympathetically. Mollie was one of the many widows that the War had created, but she had been fortunate enough to meet and be courted by Rob Parker when he came to Wolf Creek after the War. And Logan had to admit that he had shown due concern for both his adopted son, Tommy Brewster, and his own son, Kenny, whenever he had consulted Logan about an ailment. He reassured her and got on with the rest of his rounds.

After he had seen his last patient, he went to Isabella's Restaurant on Washington Street and ate a hearty meal before heading to The Eldorado Saloon. He was in time to catch the tail end of the Du Pree Players' first act. He enjoyed a drink at the end of the bar with Virgil Calhoun, the stout, jovial owner, whose ingrowing toenail he had removed the week before.

The saloon was full. The air was full of banter and raucous laughter following the first part of the Du Pree Players' show. One week a month, Howard Du Pree and his partner Eddie Foyle were the house entertainers. They had another five members who brought a range of skills and talents, including singing, dancing, and a bit of conjuring, juggling and fire-eating. But the things that they prided themselves on most were their risqué excerpts from the works of William Shakespeare. Eddie Foyle, whose female impersonations were so good that he was not infrequently propositioned by a drunken customer –much to the chagrin of several of the dance girls who felt they had been slighted in the process –felt that it was their way of bringing culture to the west.

The audience had shuffled away from the elevated stage after laughing themselves raw as the players performed a pastiche of *The Taming of the Shrew*, in which the henpecked husband –played by the tall beanpole Howard Du Pree –turned on the shrew, played to perfection by Foyle, bending 'her' over his knee and delivering a noisy spanking with the flat of his hand. Clearly, it was a performance that struck a chord with many in the audience, if they only had the gumption to confront their own sweet shrews.

Logan had seen the play performed at the Lyceum Theatre in London many years before, but had to admit that the Du Pree version was far more comedic and better suited to a very mixed Wolf Creek clientele.

"You sure are a wizard with that scalpel and those tong things of yours, Doc," Virgil Calhoun said in his South Carolina drawl, as he brought the conversation round to his favorite topic – himself. "When you wrapped that rubber tube around my toe I thought you were going to maybe lop the blasted thing off. I don't mind telling you that it was hurting me like hell. Who would have thought that a darned toenail could dig in and cause so much pain?"

Bob Sutton the bartender, a gangly middle aged fellow with a grin as toothy as his boss's, wiped spilled beer from the counter in front of them and sucked air in though his teeth. "I can't say I'd care for that, Doc. What do you use them tongs for?"

"They're called forceps, Bob," Logan returned with a grin. "I just stop the blood supply with a length of rubber tube that I wrap round the toe, then I take a small wedge of nail away before I shove one blade of the forceps down behind the nail." He held up his own left thumb and made gestures with the first two fingers of his right hand to illustrate how the procedure was done. "Then we clip it and yank the whole nail out. It's a bit like pulling a tooth, really."

Bob Sutton grimaced and went pale as a sheet. He turned to Virgil. "My jaw ached for a week when that drunk dentist Doc Cantrell pulled one of my back teeth," he said, gingerly touching his cheek. "Do you mind if I help myself to a snifter, boss? I reckon that's the worst thing I could think of. I feel like I might keel over."

"Worst blamed excuse I ever heard you come out with for a free drink," replied Virgil Calhoun with a shake of his head. Then magnanimously, "Go on, then, before the doc has another patient."

Logan grinned and turned to lean his back against the bar counter. The dance girls were ambling about, smiles fixed and their charms all too clearly visible, while one of the Du Pree Players bashed out a medley of musical favorites to keep the punters in the mood for entertainment. All three gambling tables were in action as the Wolf Creek hardened gamblers strove to beat Lady Luck at poker, faro and monte.

"Human nature never fails to amaze me, Virgil," Logan mused. "All of these men work their hides off in one way or another to earn enough dollars to live. Then they come here, play whatever game takes their fancy, and eventually hand their money over to Tom Scroggins or one of your other dealers. And that effectively means to you."

Virgil Calhoun grinned as he hooked a thumb into each pocket of his vest. "Well now, that is just the way that the world works, Logan. Each to his own, I always say. People have certain desires and I provide means for them to satisfy them. I make sure that the games are honest, which is as fair as I can be. What is wrong with me making a living out of it?"

Logan sipped his whiskey. "No harm at all Virgil. I was just wondering. It seems to me that gamblers are a pretty mixed bunch. You have professionals who make a good living out of it, a lot who dabble but know when they have had enough, and then you have the ones who will bet on anything at all, be willing to lose their last cent on the turn of a card or the roll of the dice."

"The last type are the ones I pray for," laughed Virgil.

Logan scanned the players at the various tables. "Have you had a smooth-looking gambling man in here this week? Smart clothes, goatee beard and a wooden leg?"

The saloon owner stroked his chin, pensively. "As a matter of fact we have. Poker player and pretty darned good. He was a professional, no mistakes. And according to Tom and some of the other boys, he's been around the other places. As if he was working out which would be the best to settle down at. Trouble is, all of the places have their own regular gamblers. They can be a territorial bunch, and things could get tough for a peg legged tinhorn." He finished his own drink and set his glass down on the counter. "Why, do you know him?"

Logan smiled. "Only professionally." He drained his drink before setting the glass down beside Virgil's. "I was expecting him to call to see me for a supply of medicine, but he never showed up. I wondered if he had left town."

"Could well have done. It's been a couple of days since he showed up here," Virgil replied, raising his hand to catch Bob Sutton's attention. "Have another drink."

"No, I need to hit the sack. I never know when I'll be called out at the moment."

He left as the Du Pree Players returned to the stage with a rousing fanfare.

***

It was sometime after three o'clock in the morning when Logan was woken from a light sleep. The rapping at the door was rapid, but fairly faint, rousing Logan's suspicion that it was a child rather than a grown-up who was demanding his attention in the night.

It was Tommy Brewster, and he looked like a frightened jackrabbit.

"My ma and pa sent me, Dr. Munro. It's my baby brother. He's sick and has that cough again. Can you come quick?"

Logan was used to dressing and dashing out in a hurry. "You go on home, Tommy. I'll be following you in a few moments."

True to his word, two minutes later he was hurrying along Washington Street towards the far end of town where the Parker house looked out over Wolf Creek.

He knocked on the door and immediately let himself in. In the dim light from the oil lamp he saw Rob Parker's big bulk sitting in a chair with his back to him.

Curiously, there was no telltale cough from Kenny Parker.

He noticed that Rob Parker's head was slumped forward and he saw rope wound round him and the chair.

The hairs on the back of his neck suddenly stood on end, as if some sixth sense was alerting him to danger.

But it was too late. There was an explosive pain at the back of his head and he felt himself pitching forward into a deep pool of unconsciousness.

\*\*\*

Someone was whistling. And alongside the whistling there seemed to be a muffled moaning.

Logan struggled to force his eyes to open. Then he was aware of a feeling of nausea, and of a throbbing headache, worse than any he had ever experienced before in his life.

His vision was blurred, but slowly he became able to focus in the dim lamplight. Still the whistling went on, a cheerful tune, as if someone was pleased about something.

Then he saw Mollie Parker and young Tommy Brewster bound and gagged, propped up on the bed. Their eyes stared at him in horror and he could see that they were both shaking with fear. Baby Kenny seemed to be sleeping peacefully in his basket beside Mollie.

"What…what is…?" he mumbled. Then he gasped as he saw Rob Parker's large bulk lying on his back on the old table. A stout rope was wound round and round him and the table, securing him tightly. Logan could see the look of terror on his face. A deep gash on the side of his head had bled and soaked a linen rag that had been used to gag him.

The whistling stopped and was replaced by a soft laugh.

Logan turned his head and saw Barclay Patterson sitting just out of the circle of lamplight on the other side of the bed. In his hand he had a gun trained on the doctor, and in the other he held an unsheathed swordstick.

"Why, Dr. Munro. We are so pleased that you could join us," he said, silkily. "Now we are all united again." He pointed the sword at the chair by the stove.

71

"Please take a seat and make yourself comfortable. I think it is time we all had a chat, before we begin."

Conscious of the gun that was unerringly aimed at his chest, Logan rose and sat down on the chair.

"Before we begin what?" he asked.

"Let's call it the re-union. Rob Parker here and me go back a long ways, don't we, Rob?" He gave a short laugh. "Or rather, don't we –*Chris.*"

He glanced at Mollie Parker then shook his head slowly. "I am sorry if the news that your husband isn't who he says he is comes as a surprise, but if it is a surprise, I warn you there is worse to come. This is Chris Bodeen, the worst friend a man could ever meet."

Rob Parker shook his head vigorously and made muffled protests.

"What's that, Chris? You disagree? Well, we'll hear what you say in a minute, right after I tell the folks here all about you. But when I do untie that gag, be warned. If you or Dr. Munro here make any attempt to call for help, I'll kill young Tommy and Mollie first." He swished the sword through the air. "I've become pretty handy with this here weapon."

"Chris and I fought for the Union during the war. Actually, 'fought' may not be quite right, because we had a neat line in bounty jumping. Thanks to the Union we got paid three hundred dollars to enlist, which we did, then took a sort of holiday before we re-enlisted again someplace else. We did that twelve or thirteen times each."

He laid the sword down on the edge of the bed for a moment, then drew out a small bottle of laudanum and took a swig, all the time keeping the gun trained on Logan.

"That's better. It goes right to the spot. Now where was I? Ah yes, our bounty jumping. We were friends, shared everything, and even intended buying a ranch together when it was all over. Until we had the misfortune to enlist and run into Sergeant Oliver Brewster. He knew there was something odd going on and kept a watchful eye on us, which we didn't take too kindly to.

"One day he took us on a scouting detail and told us that he knew what we were up to. We thought he was going to turn us in, but instead he demanded half of our stash. He had been listening to us in the barracks and threatened to turn us in, which of course could have meant the rope or a firing squad. Chris kept him talking long enough for me to shove a bayonet between his ribs."

He glanced at Mollie and Tommy, his eyes cold and hard and his face beaming, as if relishing their reactions of fear and horror.

"There was nothing more to be done except make another run for it and maybe enlist someplace else. I started off, and then Chris here had an attack of conscience or something. When I started off he shot me and then knocked me out."

He sighed and then fixed his stare on Logan. "The next thing I remember was you! Standing over me with your apron all bloody and a great long knife in your hand and a whole bunch of saws and such-like on a table at your side. You mumbled something about having to take my leg off to save my life. Then some bastard put a cone over my face and I blotted out. Except I felt that cold, cold steel as you cut, then that rasping as you sawed, and then the

73

smell, that goddamned awful smell of my own flesh being burned."

Logan strained to remember Barclay Patterson in army uniform, but he couldn't. There had been so many young wounded men that he had to operate on in the field hospitals. Each one of them had been a life or death operation.

"I am sorry, but I do not remember," Logan began. "I…"

"You were the one who is responsible for this damned pain in my ghost leg! And you are going to pay for it."

Rob Parker had started to strain against his bonds.

"Ah, I said you could have your say, didn't I, Chris?" Patterson rose from his chair with practiced ease. He crossed the room to the table, leaned the sword against it and reached down for Logan's medical bag. He opened it with one hand, peered inside, and then drew out Logan's Beaumont-Adams revolver.

"No sense in tempting you, doctor," he said. He stowed the weapon in a pocket of his coat, before reaching into the bag again and drawing out a small wooden case. He opened it with one hand and beamed as he removed a small scalpel from it. He inserted the blade under Rob Parker's gag and cut it free.

"Zeke, I swear I never meant any harm," Rob Parker gasped. "It wasn't how you think. I saved your life."

"Pah! Lies! Remember what I said about trying to summon help. You have one minute to tell us your side."

Rob Parker looked beseechingly at Mollie and Tommy Brewster, then turned back to look up at the man he called Zeke.

"It's true what Zeke says, we were a couple of bounty jumpers, but I wanted no part in the murder. I was trying to talk Sergeant Brewster around when Chris…when you stabbed him. Then I tried to stop you when you set off. As sure as hell we would have been hanged as murderers. But you wouldn't listen. I reckoned the only way was to wound you, take you back to the line and say we'd been ambushed and the sergeant killed. That's why I shot you in the leg then knocked you out. There was no other way I could carry you.

"I got you back and then a couple of guys from the ambulance corps took you by stretcher you to the hospital. The trouble was the Minié ball was designed to cause maximum damage. I…I guess it did it to your leg."

The man called Zeke tapped the end of his sword against his chest. "I carry the damned thing in a pouch that I keep hung round my neck." He glowered at Logan. "This damned surgeon put it in my hand as some sort of souvenir."

Logan sighed. "Those were difficult times, Mr. Patterson. Hard decisions had to be made on the spur of the moment. Having some tangible object like a bullet that maimed you often seemed to help men. If they could accept that it hadn't killed them, but only wounded them, then they could use it as a sort of talisman, a lucky charm."

Barclay Patterson laughed. "So that is the secret of my success at poker!" Then his face hardened. "I made an oath when I eventually came back to something like

75

normal consciousness. They told me that I had raved for days on end and almost died from some fever. I vowed that I would hunt down and kill the butcher that did this to me as well as the bastard who shot me."

He laughed again. "Imagine my surprise when I landed up in Wolf Creek and find the surgeon holed up as the town doctor. I guess I fainted when I saw you, because I wanted to just kill you right there. And then you went on about your oath and I thought I would need to savor the moment before I kept the oath I had made to kill you. Then Lady Luck must have smiled on me, because the first saloon I walked into, who should be there serving beer, but old Chris. Of course it's been a few years, and with this beard I guess I don't look like the same man, so I was pleased that you didn't recognize me."

He turned to the bartender. "And I see you've set yourself up and have a family and all. You married Sergeant Brewster's widow and had a sprog of your own, too. I reckon that must have been guilt that made you seek her out."

"Please, let them go, Zeke. Kill me if you want to, but just let them go."

"If you and the good doctor do as I say then maybe I'll let them live."

He picked up a bottle of whiskey from the floor and pulled out the cork. "You're going to have a good long drink, Chris. You're going to need it."

He shoved the bottle to Rob Parker's lips and forced him to drink.

"All of it! You're going to need it all."

\*\*\*

76

"I won't do it!" Logan said a few minutes later, when Barclay Paterson's intention became clear. He looked down at the contents of his medical bag that Patterson had placed at the side of the table next to the nearly comatose Rob Parker. "It is against the Hippocratic Oath. I cannot and will not do anything to willfully harm a patient."

Patterson shrugged. "It is the only way that anyone is going to walk out of here alive. It is nothing to me. I can kill you all and be off on that horse that I have ready behind the house – or you can save everyone. All you have to do is amputate his right arm. And since I am such a fair man, you chopped my leg off below the knee, so I'll allow you to take his arm off below his elbow."

"I can't. It's…it's inhuman!"

"He'll barely feel a thing. Now get out those instruments and explain to me exactly how you carry out this operation. I'm curious to know what you do and just how you deal with the two bones in the forearm."

Logan bit his lip. There seemed to be no other way to have any chance of stopping the carnage that would take place otherwise. He was already deeply concerned about the effect all of this horror would have on the young Tommy Brewster.

He opened the amputation case that he always carried in his medical bag. "I'll need to heat these cautery irons to seal off the blood vessels," he said, selecting two long metal instruments with wooden handles.

He opened up the stove and raked the wood inside to get a blaze going, then inserted the cautery irons.

"First, I'll need to apply a tourniquet to his upper arm to cut off the blood supply, then I need a short scalpel to cut through the skin down to the muscles. I always try to use the flap amputation technique. That means the incision is done obliquely round the arm rather than in a circle, which will allow me to keep a flap to cover the stump. "

He selected the instruments one by one and placed them in a row. "Then I'll need a bistoury knife, that's this long one with the curved blade. I'll use that to separate the muscles down to the bone. I'll also need this tenaculum to pinch the end of arteries and catgut to tie them off and stitch the muscles' ends."

He opened a small jar and drew out a strip of linen, which he cut upwards from one end with a pair of scissors, so that it had three tails.

"I'll use this to retract the muscles back from the bones," he explained. "One strip goes between the radius and the ulna bones and the others go round them so that I can pull the muscles back to give me a sight of the bones. Then I'll need that medium bone-saw."

Barclay Patterson tossed the empty whiskey bottle aside, the contents of which he had forced Rob Parker to drink. "Right, Dr. Munro. Then I suggest you start operating. He looks about out of it."

"Let me put a wood splint between his teeth, this will hurt like hell when I start cutting into skin."

As he did so he looked pleadingly at Patterson. "I ask you, man to man, don't subject Mrs. Parker and Tommy to this."

The gambler's fist tightened on the gun in his hand and he shook his head. "Start cutting."

Logan applied the tourniquet to Rob Parker's upper arm and screwed it tight until the veins stood out on the forearm and the skin started to change.

"I'll have to move quickly," he said, placing the scalpel against the arm. "Whiskey is no substitute for chloroform."

He quickly incised the skin in a rapid oblique circle all the way round the mid-forearm.

He heard the rapid intake of breath from the bed and imagined Mollie Parker and Tommy Brewster fainting, but he had no time to look.

Barclay Patterson laughed eerily as Rob Parker's eyes shot open and his body bucked against the ropes that restrained him.

"Excellent work, doctor. Pray continue."

Logan reached for the sharp, long-bladed bistoury knife. "I warn you, there will be a lot of blood with this. I have to go deep and I'll be cutting through his radial and ulnar arteries. The tourniquet will have stopped most of the supply, but you can never completely cut it off.'"

"Go on! Cut! Cut!"

Logan wiped the perspiration from his brow with the back of his hand. He moved his hand slowly up across his forehead, then rapidly kept moving upwards, at the same time spinning round to throw the bistoury with all his might. It flew like an arrow and pierced Barclay Patterson's right eye all the way to the hilt. There was an accompanying sickening squelch and crackle as it went through orbital contents and orbital cavity into the brain. Blood and yellow eye jelly spurted out.

The gun went off as the gambler's body toppled forward and crashed to the floor where it began convulsing, the wooden leg beating an horrific, macabre staccato noise on the floor.

Then he lay motionless. Immediately, Logan bent and felt his neck, searching for the carotid pulse. He was dead.

To his great relief, he saw that both Mollie and Tommy had indeed passed out and had been spared the spectacle of the man's grisly death. He released them and lay them gently on the bed, sure that they would recover and need his aid in moments. But first he needed to tend Rob Parker, who was lapsing in and out of consciousness, struggling to overcome the effect of the bottle of whiskey.

Logan set about stitching the incision on his arm before releasing the tourniquet, so that he had a relatively bloodless field on which to work. It was only then that he started to even consider what would have happened had he missed the throw with the bistoury knife. It had been a gamble, pure and simple. Fortunately, it had paid off.

As he stitched, he considered how he was going to get Marshal Gardner over here. He didn't envy the task the lawman would face in sorting out the aftermath of this case.

Like Logan, Gardner had taken an oath; only his was to uphold the law. In a way Logan was relieved that as a humble doctor he was only required to care for his patients. In saving them from Barclay Patterson he had done just that. He felt no qualms about the way the gambler died. Indeed, it gave him some professional satisfaction, not unlike the feeling he got whenever he relieved pain by letting pus out of a festering abscess.

He wondered how many cases of festering hatred the War had produced.

THE END

## IT TAKES A MAN
### by
### Cheryl Pierson

Derrick McCain let go a low curse as he finished saddling his dun, then turned toward the roan his mother would be riding.

He should have gone back a long time ago, Derrick thought. Right after he found out whose son he truly *was* – not the man he'd always thought of as his father…and that was a blessing.

The grim-faced Cherokee messenger, Austenaco Little Horse, stood stoically in the corner of the barn, watching. Derrick could feel his old childhood friend's thrumming impatience from across the room.

Austen had appeared on their doorstep in the middle of this November night, apparently expecting them to be ready to ride with no more than five minutes' notice.

Derrick's father –his *real* father –was sick. He pressed his lips together as he remembered the words Austen had spoken.

"Collin Ridge requests you come at once –with no further delay." There'd been a slight emphasis on the word *further*, and Derrick knew it was aimed at him. Yet, his mother had looked down quickly when the words had been spoken –as if she felt their sting in her conscience, as well.

"We must hurry," Austen urged, and Derrick couldn't help but wonder if things were even more dire than his longtime friend had led them to believe. Of course, for Austen to knock on the door in the darkness of night, things had to be pretty bad from the outset, he reminded himself. He tried to put a lid on his temper, knowing that a big part of his short fuse was due to his own anger at himself –and in not having gone back to Indian Territory sooner, before his father had had to summon him to his sickbed.

Derrick finished saddling the gentle roan in silence, not answering Austen's prodding. It would take a few minutes to prepare everything they'd need to take –and everything that had to be left behind, as well, since there was no way of knowing how long they'd be away.

"I'm ready," Fiona McCain said from the doorway of the barn.

In the dim light of the lanterns, Derrick saw that his mother carried a small duffel bag of provisions and another containing what he could only surmise was clothing and personal items that a woman might need. Her eyes were anxious with a mixture of worry and anticipation. It had been over seventeen years since she'd seen Derrick's father –the man who still held her heart.

Yet, even though Derrick had tried to confront her with the knowledge of his parentage, she'd put him off, not wanting or allowing an honest conversation between them. Derrick had tried twice –the first time had been several months ago when he'd come home from chasing Jim Danby's gang into the San Bois Mountains –just after he'd learned the truth.

Fiona had pulled him to her and hugged him, saying simply, "I'm so glad you're home safe, Derrick." Then she'd gone to cook dinner, dodging the questions he put to her.

A few months later, his sister, Kathleen had been kidnapped by Danby's surviving cutthroats, who now followed Clark Davis. Again, he'd broached the subject a few days after his return, and again, Fiona had sidestepped the questions as elegantly as a dance master teaching a novice the steps to a waltz.

Now, only weeks from that aborted conversation, here they were, preparing to travel several days of hard riding to get to a man that his mother refused to discuss.

*Why?*

"We can stop by Kathleen's on the way out of town and let her know to come see to the livestock," Fiona said calmly. "Give me a hand up, son. It's been a while since I rode Betsy."

Derrick laced his fingers together and Fiona stepped into his palms, boosting herself up into the saddle. She looped the drawstrings of the bags securely around the saddle horn and rode out of the barn without looking back.

Austen shook his head. "She's just like I remembered, Derrick." A faint grin touched his mouth. "She hasn't changed. And neither have you."

Derrick blew out the lamps, leading his horse to the door. Austen walked beside Derrick into the darkness.

"Yeah, Austen, I've changed." He swung up into the saddle as Austen did. "Seventeen years –no way a man can stay the same that long."

"Not in the middle of a war," Austen agreed.

But there was more than the war, Derrick thought. And more than the passage of time. *There was finding out you weren't who you thought you were.*

Derrick remained silent, turning his horse southward, toward the outskirts of Wolf Creek, toward what had once been his home...Indian Territory.

\*\*\*

Five days later, they rode into the small settlement of Porum, Indian Territory –in the Cherokee Nation, but inhabited mostly by Anglos. The late afternoon sun colored the buildings like a painting, and Derrick was struck by the changes that had taken place in the years since his family had left there.

Fiona had drawn Betsy up on the rise. Her gaze swept over the activity below, and even farther beyond, where the Cherokee village of Briartown lay.

Her breathing hitched, and she squared her shoulders before starting forward once more. In that gesture, Derrick realized how uncertain his mother was about the wisdom of what she was about to do. Yet, there was no choice –not for either of them.

Austen wisely said nothing, his dark stare penetrating, meeting Derrick's own for a moment, then sliding away from scrutiny.

They rode down from the top of the ridge into the settlement. Many of the original buildings were still here, Derrick noticed, as well as several new additions and expansions. Obviously, the community was thriving, though it looked to be smaller than Wolf Creek.

No one spared them a second glance. Fiona rode slowly, and Derrick wondered if she was hoping to see a familiar face among the people on the streets.

Derrick looked at the faces, too, but for a different reason. The unexpected appearance of Jim Danby's gang in Wolf Creek had taught him a lesson he'd never forget. No matter where he went, now, he'd always look for faces from his past. Circumstances had changed in his life, and he wasn't about to let the man he'd once been catch up with the man he had become. It had taken too long to reconcile the two.

Anxiety clawed at his insides. What would they find in Briartown? Would his true father already have died? He wanted badly for this reunion to take place, and selfishly, not because of what it might mean to his mother.

He'd spent a lifetime knowing he was different somehow, never fitting in with his family. Charley Blackfeather, the Seminole scout, had commented often on his "Cherokee face" –so often, in fact, that Charley called him *Cherokee* rather than by his given name.

When they'd pursued Danby's gang only a few months past, Derrick had run into someone who had solved the puzzle –an old childhood friend from his days in Indian Territory. Carson Ridge had told him the bittersweet truth –he and Derrick were half-brothers, both sons of the Cherokee statesman, Collin Ridge.

Derrick glanced sideways at his mother. She was still a beautiful woman, despite the hardships she'd faced. Had she ever been in love with her husband, Andrew McCain? His sister, Kathleen, had spoken of a letter she'd found in Fiona's jewelry casket –a letter that their mother had written to her husband. In it, she'd spoken of her love for Collin Ridge and the son that belonged to them – Derrick. She'd written of dreams that had never come true, and of her wish to go back to Briartown and re-establish a relationship with Ridge, the man she loved. But, she'd

86

never done that –even after Andrew McCain's death. *Why not?*

She must have loved Collin beyond anything, to risk an illicit affair with him. She'd become pregnant with Derrick. He'd always felt the difference of his parentage, and had never been close to his brothers or the man he thought of as his father. What could she have done? She'd been trapped, just as he had been.

As Derrick watched her, now, he sensed anticipation, along with the insecurity that anyone in her situation would feel. Still, Ridge wouldn't have sent for her had he not wished to see her, to speak with her.

*And him*, Derrick thought. What could a father say to a grown son? A flash of envy shot through Derrick as he thought of the conversations he and his half-brother, Carson, had had this past summer. So many misunderstandings and deceit had nearly burned a bridge that Derrick hadn't even known existed.

*Why hadn't he gone back sooner? Once he'd known, what had held him in Wolf Creek?*

Surely, his father must be wondering the same thing…

His thoughts cleared as they neared the end of the Main Street shops, and the horses and conveyances became easier to navigate. They headed out onto the open plains once more, toward Briartown. A small enough distance separated the Anglo settlement of Porum from the Cherokee one of Briartown; an ocean of distance –and *difference* –inside his own chest at the knowledge that he had a foot planted in both worlds, now.

As they closed the gap, Derrick began to think of the things he wanted to say to Collin Ridge. For words of needing and hoping, the time was past. Regret for what he'd missed would always be with him. But now, there might be time to look toward a future, and a heritage he'd not claimed.

*If he dared.*

\*\*\*

They rode into the village, Fiona's head raised proudly as she met the eyes of some of the women she had known before, when her husband had been the headmaster at the Cherokee school.

The three of them were an open curiosity. It was clear to Derrick that the entire population must know that Ridge had sent Austenaco for them. Again, that feeling of not belonging washed over him. He thought of his friend, Charley Blackfeather, a half-breed of a different sort. But where Charley had been raised, half-Black, half-Seminole had been *accepted*. Here, with the Cherokees, Derrick would have been accepted, as well. In the white world, half-anything would never be more than tolerated.

Derrick tried to settle into his own skin as well as he could under the circumstances. At least he was not in any danger here.

They stopped in front of Collin Ridge's large wood cabin, where Austen and Derrick dismounted. Derrick helped Fiona down, her eyes meeting his. There was an awkward silence, and she started to speak, but then decided against it.

"You will go in first, Mrs. McCain, and we will wait at my home," Austen said, giving Derrick a quick look. "This, according to Mr. Ridge's wishes."

"Certainly," Fiona murmured. She started for the door, climbing the three steps to the veranda. Before she knocked, she turned back to look at Derrick. "Your questions will all be answered soon, Derrick."

At that moment, the door swung open, and Rella, Ridge's youngest daughter, greeted Fiona somberly, her gaze taking Derrick and Austen in as they stood beside their mounts.

"Father will see Mrs. McCain alone first."

Fiona walked into the house, the door shutting behind her with a soft click. There was nothing to do now but wait.

\*\*\*

"Hungry?" Austen asked. There was amusement in his tone, and when Derrick turned to look at him, the warm light of laughter shone in his dark eyes. "If you're not yet, you will be before Ridge will see you."

Derrick raised a brow, and Austen laughed. "You didn't think they'd catch up on over seventeen years of separation in the blink of an eye, did you, Derrick? Ridge's wife passed over two years ago. McCain has passed, as well. There is nothing standing in their way any longer."

Derrick bristled, stepping closer to his old friend. "What the hell does *that* mean?"

Austen shook his head. "Come on. You can eat with us tonight. You and I haven't talked much on this journey. You've been...preoccupied."

Derrick gave a low laugh. "*Rude*, you mean. I'm sorry, Austen."

Austen started walking, and Derrick fell into step with him.

"I married Josie Martin –do you remember her?" He went on without waiting for a response. "We have three children, and a fourth on the way."

"Josie Martin…" Derrick mused. "Haven't seen her since she was a kid. She was younger than Kathleen!"

Austen gave him a wounded look. "Only by a year!"

Derrick laughed again. "So you're a family man, now, Austen?" Derrick couldn't help but think of how wild Austenaco Little Horse had been as a young boy; a daredevil, willing to do just about anything.

Austen smiled, leading his horse down the rough street toward his home. "Yes, I'm a *family man*, as you call it." He fell silent a moment before he went on. "I had demons inside my soul, from the time I was very young. But somehow, Josie quiets them and eases my path in life. She's younger in years than I am, but older in her wise way. It was she who came to me with a marriage proposal."

"She must've gotten tired of waiting," Derrick said.

Austen grinned. "That's just what she said to me. She was in love with me and wanted a life together; that I needed to stop thinking of her as a child."

Derrick's lips quirked. "And then?"

"And then…" Austen stopped, turning to look at Derrick, "she showed me how much of a woman she was."

He started walking again. "We were married the next week."

"Congratulations. You seem...happy."

Austen stopped in front of a small house. "I am." His eyes bored into Derrick's. "Josie saved my life, in a way. There's no telling what might have happened to me without her."

"And your children –"

"Let me tell you something, Derrick. Each of my children is different. Each one is special. I love them all, but in ways that are different. Mary is the eldest. Her beauty shines in her eyes. Her spirit is steadfast and unwavering. Benjamin, my son, is two years younger. He's much like I was –he reminds me of me." He gave a wry laugh. "But I understand him. And I know how he thinks. He would give his life for his family. His loyalty knows no limits."

"Again, like you." Derrick had not forgotten the way Austen had jumped to his defense on more than one occasion, even though he had been a couple of years older than Derrick.

"Yes. It is a good quality –and one that is undervalued at times."

"What of your youngest?"

Austen's face sobered. "Sarah. She is the scholar in our family. As young as she is, she is learning the history of our people; the stories and customs that we must keep alive." Austen glanced at the door. "Come. I'll have Benjamin see to our horses. Josie will be glad to see you again."

The door opened as Austen and Derrick stepped forward, and there was an eruption of excitement as the house emptied. Austen's three children raced out to greet him joyfully. Behind them, Josie stood on the porch, very pregnant, and Austen hurried toward her to keep her from coming down the steps.

But it was the other woman who stood quietly behind Josie, to the left, who made Derrick's heart race, his breathing all but stop.

She was taller than Josie, but there was no doubt they were related. They had the same beautiful glow in their eyes, the same gentle smile.

Derrick stood back, not wanting to intrude on Austen's reunion with his family. Austen murmured something quietly to Josie and she glanced at Derrick, her smile widening.

"Come here, Derrick McCain," she called to him in Cherokee. "You've changed since you've been gone from us."

Derrick smiled. "So have you, Josie." He came forward slowly. "When I left, you were one of the pesky children we were always trying to dodge."

Josie pecked Austen on the cheek as he put an arm around her. "Yes. This one finally slowed down enough for me to catch up with him."

Austen sighed in mock resignation. "And look at me now, Derrick. Just miserable."

Josie laughed lightly, reaching to hug Derrick briefly as he came up onto the porch, then turned back to her husband. "I've got stew ready and I just made fresh fry bread. Maybe that will help you forget your misery, eh, Austen?"

Austen laughed. "I'm sure it will."

As Derrick's gaze went to the young woman behind Josie, Austen hurried to introduce them. "Derrick, this is Josie's cousin, Leah Martin. I don't think you two have met –"

Derrick put out a hand to take hers. "No. I would've remembered."

"As would I," she answered softly, with no hint of coyness.

Her hand rested in Derrick's for a moment longer than might have been proper, cool and soft. He had to stop himself from letting go abruptly when he recognized the playful reproach in her eyes. She subtly moved her fingers and he released them gradually.

"I'm pleased to make your acquaintance, ma'am."

"Thank you, Mr. McCain."

Austen held the door open for Josie and Leah. As Derrick walked through, he gave his old friend a sideways glance. Austen wore a slight smirk that Derrick recognized, but he said nothing. The two little girls clung to their father, and Austen spoke swiftly to Benjamin, instructing him to take care of their mounts before picking up his youngest and carrying her inside, his big hand on Mary's shoulder.

After the men washed up, they returned to the table to find large bowls of stew set out along with the fresh fry bread. Derrick sat across from Austen, the aroma of the stew so savory he wasn't sure he could wait for it to cool.

93

He hadn't been this hungry in a long time, and he realized a big part of that was feeling so welcome –so at home. He was accepted here. Leah and Josie sat at the table, though they had already eaten.

"How was your journey?" Josie asked.

Austen nodded as he wiped his mouth. "It was good. Too long away from you though."

She blushed, turning to look at Derrick. "And what of you, Derrick? What has happened since you left us so many years ago?"

He looked up, wondering how to answer that. He'd been packed up and taken from a whole other family that belonged to him; only, he hadn't known it at the time. He'd been cheated of so much.

"I –uh –finished my schooling, of course."

"Of course." Josie turned to Leah. "Derrick's fath – Mr. McCain was the headmaster at the Cherokee school here," she explained.

"I see." Leah took a sip of water from her cup and set it back upon the table.

"And then, when –my father was murdered by a band of damn Jayhawkers, I felt I needed to go off to war and fight for the Confederacy like my brothers, Benton and Eli. All I could think of was revenge."

"Vengeance for the Bluecoats, you mean?" Leah asked. "Because your family were Southern sympathizers?"

Derrick gave a short laugh. "No. More for finding those men that killed my father. But I fell in with a group I…would've been better off without."

"A gang?" Leah questioned with interest. "One of those groups of border outlaws?"

Derrick nodded, then took another bite of stew, trying to think of how to reply to that. The censure in her tone said he had sunk as low as those who had murdered Andrew McCain in cold blood. *He had not ever done that.* Somehow, he's always managed to keep that part of his conscience clean –almost, finally, at the cost of his own life. The men he'd killed had needed it.

Conversation fell silent. Derrick looked up into Leah's steady black-eyed gaze. "I've killed. I've *had* to. But the men who died by my hand were out to kill me and the men I fought with, ma'am. That's how war is."

"And...afterward? The border raiders you joined – weren't they the same type of men who killed your father?" There was a hint of challenge in her voice.

Derrick answered it swiftly.  She had no idea what it had taken from him to ride with those men, and how it had nearly cost him everything. "Yeah. Nearly got killed myself when I refused to do what you're talkin' about."

"Derrick healed up and came back to Wolf Creek to take care of the farm," Austen put in quickly, steering the conversation back to safer ground. "When some of those men showed up and raided the town, he joined the posse to go after them."

"What happened?" Josie exclaimed.

"We got most of 'em," Derrick said. He would've left it at that, but Austen spoke up again.

"One of them got away and put a new gang together. They kidnapped Kathleen."

95

Josie gasped, glancing at her cousin. "Derrick's sister," she said, in quick explanation.

Leah leaned forward. "Did you –were you able to rescue her?"

Derrick smiled, pushing his chair away from the table. "Yeah. We got her back."

"They are wicked, cruel men." Leah put her hand to her throat. "I'm so glad she wasn't harmed. Or you, either."

*No need to correct that misconception. The scars had healed, for the most part. Let her think what she would. It didn't matter anyway.*

Josie said, "Derrick, I'm sorry about the deaths of your –of Mr. McCain and your brothers."

Derrick nodded. "Thank you. You know, I wasn't close to them, but still…" His voice trailed off and he looked away. "I suppose it's anybody's guess as to why Collin Ridge has asked to see my mother and me after all this time." He watched each of them closely. There was a flicker in Austen's eyes before he glanced down. Derrick went on. "Aside from the fact that he's dying."

"Come, Leah, let's wash up these dishes." Josie stood abruptly, and reluctantly, Leah followed. It was clear this was a conversation for the men alone, one she did not want to miss.

"Let's go outside," Austen said.

"Papa –" Sarah started.

Austen knelt and gave his daughter a quick kiss. "You wait for me. I'll be back in a few minutes."

She nodded and turned away.

Derrick walked to the door, waiting for Austen. A shot of envy went through him, unfamiliar and surprising in its intensity. He'd never wanted children. But ever since he'd come here with Austen, he'd gotten a feeling of coming home. And the closeness between Austen and his family set up a yearning in Derrick that he'd never acknowledged before. It played on the hurt that had been an open wound all his life between his 'father' and him; the constant feeling of not fitting anywhere within his own family. Once again, his life was in turmoil. It seemed he was doomed either to be courting death or dying slowly of the boredom of a routine he despised. Farming was not what he'd expected from his life.

But…what *did* he want? Surely not the solitary existence he'd led as a young boy, feeling separated somehow from everyone and everything. Not the rigors he'd set out for when he'd joined the Confederacy, and certainly not the harshness he'd fallen into with Jim Danby's raiders.

Still, going back to Wolf Creek and trying to take over the farm and make a go of it had been excruciating in its sameness. If he knew anything, he knew he wasn't a farmer. And seeing Austen with his family made Derrick more aware than ever that his life was most likely half over and he had not one damn thing to show for it.

He opened the door with a little more force than was necessary, drawing a raised eyebrow from his old friend as he followed Derrick out onto the porch.

"Walk with me," Austen said in a firm tone. They started down toward the gentle slope of the nearby branch of Boggy River, where they had all played as youngsters.

97

After a moment, Austen spoke. "You need to find your balance."

Derrick smiled, thinking of another friend who often spoke of *balance*. Charley. "Easier said than done."

Austen nodded. "Yes, and especially hard for you, being a half blood, one foot in our culture and one in the Anglo world. This was something your mother should have told you long ago."

"It must have been a terrible *shame* to her," Derrick muttered. "That's the only reason I can think of that she didn't."

Austen's look was almost pitying as he stopped a few feet from the rushing water. "Truly? The *only* reason?"

"What else?"

"A terrible *love*, Derrick. Did you ever think that maybe she tried to forget Ridge? Because she had to leave him behind?"

"No," Derrick answered flatly.

"That's because you've never had that kind of feeling for another. If you had," Austen went on, "–you would understand." His gaze was steady, until finally Derrick turned away.

"Why not tell me, though?"

"Because then *you* would have had a choice. How could a mother choose among her children? That's why she went when your father decided to go. To arm you with the truth would have given you the power to have broken up the family...don't you see?"

Derrick gave a short laugh, turning back to face his friend. "I'm trying, Austen. But what keeps hitting me in the face is the memory of me leaving here; everything I ever knew. Leaving Carson behind –my best friend, and my *brother*."

"The path was made *for* you before. Now, it's up to you to *choose* it."

Derrick nodded. "I want to see my father."

"He'll send for you when –"

"No. I'm not going to see *the statesman*, Collin Ridge. I'm going to see my *father*."

\*\*\*

Twilight had fallen and was on the way to complete darkness as Derrick made his way down the street.

The houses clustered respectably together for most of the length of the rutted dirt road, then gave way to the businesses and finally, the saloon. The music and laughter spilled out at the end of the street, but Derrick wasn't going that far.

He stopped in front of the cabin where he'd left his mother earlier. Two kerosene lamps hung on either side of the door. *Odd, how such a tiny bit of light could seem so welcoming.*

From inside, there was a soft glow in most of the front rooms. He slowly walked up the front steps, and raised his hand to knock. Before he could, the bolt slid back from inside, and the door swung open.

He recognized another of Carson's sisters, Talita, the eldest. She smiled broadly, and he stepped forward to hug her.

"Welcome home, Derrick," she said softly.

As she stepped back to look at him, he saw the uncertainty in her face.

"It's good to be here, sister."

She hugged him again. "I'm so glad –" She broke off, as if she were afraid of saying too much.

"Where is my father?" he asked bluntly.

"He and your mother are in here." She shut the door and turned to lead him across the front room and down a small hallway, pausing to knock at the first door they came to.

"Father, you have a visitor," she called out in Cherokee.

"Send him in," a deep voice answered.

Derrick opened the door, leaving it ajar behind him. His mother rose quickly from her chair beside the bed.

"Derrick –"

"Leave us, please," he said, his eyes connecting with his father's.

"But –"

"I need some answers. I intend to get them."

Ridge motioned her out. "He's right, Fiona. It's past time for this."

Silently, she walked to the door, closing it behind her with a quiet *click*.

Derrick hesitated a moment, unsure of his next move. He tried to tamp down the happiness he felt at seeing his father –especially now that the truth was known between them.

Ridge smiled at him, looking much the same as he had seventeen years earlier, his dark eyes a mirror image of Derrick's own.

Collin Ridge looked remarkably healthy –for a man who was dying. Suspicion niggled at the back of Derrick's mind. *What, exactly, was wrong with his father?* He took a step forward as Ridge shifted in the bed to a more upright position.

"Please," his father indicated the chair with a sweeping motion of his hand. "Sit down."

After a moment, Derrick took the chair Fiona had just vacated. "Are you tired, *e do da*?"

Ridge's eyes crinkled. "You ask of my health, as you call me 'Father' for the first time." He scrutinized Derrick before continuing. "I had thought to be met with your anger."

Derrick shook his head. "I'm just…disappointed."

Ridge nodded. "I know. I've lived with disappointment –and loss –as well. My family has been incomplete. At least, when you lived among us, I saw you often. When your mother's husband realized what had happened, there was no choice for your mother. To stay with me would mean leaving your brothers and sister. The only way to keep you all together was to move with him when he left for Kansas."

"I understand that. But what I don't understand is why she never told me."

Ridge laughed. "Perhaps she believed you'd be happier not knowing."

As his father's meaning hit him, Derrick shook his head. "She wasn't ashamed of what happened between you." He didn't want to betray his sister to his mother, but things had to be dealt with. "Can we keep this between us?"

Ridge nodded. "Of course. It goes no farther than these walls."

"All right. My sister, Kathleen, found some letters in Ma's things. One was written to my fath –Andrew McCain. She explained in quite some detail, according to Kathleen, that she realized she had made a mistake in staying with him." Derrick looked down, not sure how much he should say about the other letter Kathleen had told him about. The one his mother had written to the man sitting before him. "The other letter, she'd written to *you*; she –she always loved you."

"I know that, son. I only meant –maybe your mother sought to ease the way for you in the white world by keeping your Cherokee blood from you." A faint grin curved his lips. "Though I don't know how she thought to hide it from you forever. You and Carson look so much alike. You and I –" He shook his head. "I would have known you anywhere. You remind me of myself –many years ago." He paused. "If she could have chosen a different path –stayed here with me –things would have been easier for you; so much easier. You know it is our way that our society is matrilineal. With her blood and mine, you would have had the best of both our worlds. If she had become a Cherokee citizen, as her son, you'd be one, too. You could have been a leader."

"Like you?" Derrick grinned as he spoke. "Follow in your footsteps?"

His father nodded. "Maybe with even more respect and power than I've had, son," he said softly. "But your mother couldn't stay here, and at the time...I already had a wife. I only think about what might have been if our circumstances had been otherwise. You have the heart of a leader."

Derrick was quiet. Hearing his father speak made him realize that he wasn't the only one who'd had opportunities taken from him. The wistful note in his father's voice let him understand that Collin Ridge had had some unrealized hopes and dreams that had never come to fruition, either. Finally, Derrick said, "I've lost so much. So many years –"

"We *all* have, Derrick. But now is the time to change that and to move forward."

"Now that you're –sick?" He couldn't say *dying*; to do so would allow death entry to his thoughts more strongly.

"I'm feeling better, son. Just having you and your mother here with me –it's helping."

Derrick's eyes narrowed. "I've seen a lot of dying men. You're not *too* near death's door."

Ridge smiled. "Again, that's a matter that will remain between you and me, Derrick. I'm going to make a ...full recovery...with time. You know how women like to fuss. I will not let her worry, but we need this time together."

Derrick didn't say anything.

"Your mother would not have come if I but asked her. And you –" He shifted in the bed. "Why haven't you come before now? Carson told me he'd seen you months ago –that you now knew the full story –"

Derrick shook his head. "Not all of it."

"Enough to have come before now." Ridge's words were chiding, but Derrick didn't take offense.

"I've thought of it –time and again," he admitted. "To discover that you are my father –that Carson is not only my childhood friend, but also my brother –and that I have two sisters as well…" He wasn't sure how to continue. He looked down, studying the floor. "I've done some bad things in my life, *e do da*."

Ridge moved to sit up on the edge of the bed, facing Derrick. "We all have regrets, Derrick. Can you imagine how I felt, having to allow Andrew McCain raise my son? Oh, yes, Andrew was a well-respected man in the community. He was educated. But the way he raised you and your brothers, your sister –with an iron fist –the way he tried to control your mother –Still," he went on after a moment, "it takes a man to raise another man's son. And there was no doubt you were *my* son. It was…very plain to see. Things would have been different, had your mother and I been free to follow our hearts."

"I left, first chance I got."

Ridge gave Derrick a thin smile. "I know. You were loyal to the man you thought was your father. He must have done something right, raising you, to instill that in your heart. I know he didn't treat you well, son. What I said was true. It takes a man to raise another man's son – but I should have added, 'with kindness in his heart, no matter the circumstances'."

Derrick shrugged. "Didn't seem like much of that in him at all –at least, not toward me."

Ridge looked away. "You were the son of the man he thought would steal his wife away. Not that he loved her. She was a habit with him by the time you were conceived. Just property, in a way. Even though your mother was aware of that, she knew she must go with him to keep the family together."

"But later –"

"Fiona had no choice but to stay where she was, by then, in a white community. She was a widowed white woman with a white daughter. It was too late for her to come back here, she felt. She has sacrificed everything in her life for her children, Derrick. Don't think too harshly of her."

Derrick didn't respond. Had he known sooner, his life might have been different…but would it have been *better*? He would forever be neither white nor Cherokee. It was almost worse to know for certain that he carried Indian blood. He thought of Austen and Josie and their life together. Being a half-breed meant that kind of happiness could never be his. Not that he cared, he told himself. But still, his thoughts returned to Leah, and the way she'd looked at him from across the dinner table earlier. Then, how her stare had held his when he'd talked about joining up with Danby's men. The coldness in her voice, where there had been warmth before.

"I'm offering Fiona a chance at a new life, Derrick," Ridge said quietly. He reached for the shirt that lay at the foot of the bed, pulling it on. "I want her to stay here with me. And I want your support in that."

Derrick's head came up. "Surely, at this point, you know she does whatever she wants."

"Except in the matter of protecting her children. Then, she does what she must for you…for your sister…with no thought to herself. I'm hoping she'll stay. I've always loved her, too, you know." He smiled. "I'm ready to admit that to the world…to let go of any self-pride, and put only my love for her to the center of my existence, no matter the circumstances." He paused, then said, "How I wish I could have done so many, many years ago."

"You had a family –a wife. That would have been impossible."

"Nothing is impossible, son, if you want it badly enough. But, as I say, it takes a man to see that it all comes right –to restore balance to his own existence, and to his loved ones. Now that your mother has no responsibilities for her family, I hope she'll see the time has come to fulfill her own happiness."

His father had said some things that had opened his eyes, but all this talk of emotions and the impending changes made him restless. He wanted nothing more than to be outside under the stars. The river called to him. It was the best place to think. "I…need to go," he said after a moment.

His father stood slowly, giving him a long stare. "It is a lot to take in all at once." He changed the subject abruptly. "You have met Josie's cousin, Leah?"

Derrick smiled. "At dinner."

His father quirked a brow at his tone.

Derrick gave a short laugh. "Oh, no. Not interested. That is one strong-willed female."

Ridge shrugged. "It is just as well."

"Why do you say that?"

"Love is too...complicated...for some to understand or embrace. Leah has been hurt badly."

Derrick braced a hand on the wall as his father sat once more on the edge of the bed, reaching for one of his moccasins.

"I imagine we've all suffered our losses at some point," Derrick said. "You and Ma —"

"No, this is different. Be kind to her, son." There was a stern tone in Ridge's voice. A warning.

Derrick's quick glance met his father's steady gaze. "Why? What are you getting at?"

"The men you chased...one of them took advantage of Leah. Her family has not stood by her. Her father, David, I have never liked. Now, even less."

Derrick pushed away from the support of the wall, standing straight. No wonder he'd detected something more in her questioning at the dinner table. "*Raped* her? But, how did he get close ...I mean —"

Ridge slipped on his other moccasin and tied it before he answered. "She and her younger sister were gathering berries by where the river grows wider. Near the base of the San Bois foothills."

Derrick knew the place. No more than an hour's ride from here, and no more than a full day's journey from Demon's Drop where the Danby gang —most recently led by Clark Davis —stayed in hiding year-round.

"How did she know it was one of Danby's men? Danby's dead now –"

"Yes, but the ones who followed him still ride this land to commit their acts of evil. They were led by another, one with flame-colored hair."

"Clark Davis," Derrick said. "Dead now, as well."

Ridge nodded slowly. "There will be another. And another. No matter how many of them you kill, there will always be another."

Derrick had to agree. There would never be an end to evil –but hadn't he once been a part of it himself? As much as he'd like to deny it, war brought the evil –as well as the good –out in men. *Sure seemed like he'd seen a lot more of the evil than the good.*

"If only we could have gotten to Davis a few months earlier," Derrick mused quietly. "His death didn't come soon enough to help Leah."

Ridge rose from the bed. "No. But they will not defile another."

"They?"

"There were two of them. The one with red hair and one with brown."

*Proof enough that it had been Davis himself.* It could only be, with that red hair of his. But the other could've been any number of the gang members.

Ridge stepped toward Derrick solemnly. "Leah's sister, Rachel, gave her life that day; but she also took that of her attacker. We know the other man, the red-haired man, was killed at Demon's Drop." His gaze bore steadily into Derrick's.

"My friend killed him," Derrick said, remembering the bloody scalp in Charley's hand that day.

Ridge's gaze bore steadily into Derrick's. "Your friend was right to kill Clark Davis, son. He was pure evil. Now, you should let Leah know she has nothing more to fear. You were there. You saw it. It will help her to know."

Derrick let go a low curse. He could've saved Leah's virtue and possibly Rachel's life if the showdown at Demon's Drop had only come about a little earlier. Though he'd only met Leah this evening, there seemed to be a kind of steel in her that, he thought, would be accepting of what had happened to her. But she would never forget it.

They were alike in that respect. He'd learned many lessons the hard way –lessons he would never put completely behind him.

His face warmed at the thought of Leah's questions, his answers –and what the truth was that they'd both danced around across the table from one another.

"Things have a way of resolving themselves," Ridge said, as Derrick moved toward the door.

"Yeah." Derrick gave a grim sigh. "And sometimes, they need a little push."

\*\*\*

Derrick had said his goodbyes and headed back outside into the darkness. The full moon lit the dirt street. Light spilled out of the dwellings and businesses along the way back to Austen's house.

Ahead of him, Derrick caught a flash of a bright yellow dress, the same color Leah had worn. *Was it her?* They were both close enough to Austen's home that it was

109

possible. He followed the female, and once in the bright light of the moon he could see it was, indeed, Leah.

He didn't call out to her. She was headed for the rushing river behind the rows of homes. Her long strides were steady and certain. He waited at the corner of one of the houses, watching as she slipped into the tree line with a furtive backward glance.

After a moment, he followed.

Though she moved quietly, he was able to spot her easily, a few yards in the distance. As she veered to the left, he knew where she was headed. The same place Austen had found *him* earlier that evening. But why?

As Leah neared the outcropping of stone, her steps slowed.

Derrick stopped, waiting to see what she would do. She walked out onto the rock shelf and stood staring down into the rushing water.

As she turned, her body was outlined in the moonlight, and Derrick could clearly see what she'd hidden well at the dinner table beneath her shawl.

*She was pregnant.*

She watched the churning current, mesmerized for a moment, and Derrick read her thoughts. Desperation was written across her lovely features. *She was about to do the unthinkable.* It seared him to think of the beautiful fire in her eyes guttering out forever –it seared him even more to think of having that on his conscience. He stepped out from the shadows, coming toward her at a leisurely pace.

Now, he understood the turn of the dinner conversation. Had he known her circumstances, perhaps he'd have been more circumspect in his comments.

Leah glanced up as he came closer. "What are you doing here, Mr. McCain?" She lifted her head, and Derrick could see the way she tried to push the dread of what she was about to do out of her expression. Her voice was low and almost sultry, with a forced hint of disdain.

Derrick smiled. "Carson and I used to play down here every chance we got." He stepped up onto the outcropping of rock, and Leah moved away a step, just out of his reach.

He looked around, judging which way she'd jump, if she still was determined. The look in her eyes said she was.

"Current's vicious tonight," Derrick said, nodding at the water below. "Drowning wouldn't be the way I'd choose to go. I thought you were stronger than this."

Leah gave him a long stare. "You've never been in my situation, Mr. McCain, and you never will be. Sometimes, there's …simply no choice."

Derrick lowered himself to sit on the rock, his feet hanging over the edge well above the rushing water. "I understand about having no choice, Leah. Don't ever think otherwise. Like I said earlier, there's no fighting a war without doing some things you have no say in. I never set out thinking of myself as –a *murderer* –but, I've killed."

"That's different. If you hadn't, your enemy would have slain you. War is 'kill or be killed.'"

"You're letting him take your life from beyond the grave." His voice was low, his gaze intent upon her. He put a hand up to her, looking at her with expectation, until finally, she took it and sat beside him on the rock.

"Who?" She stared straight ahead, into the moon-dappled darkness.

"Clark Davis," Derrick said quietly. "The man who raped you."

She whirled quickly to face him, but the anger was only a cover for the painful humiliation. "I should slap your face for daring to –"

"To speak the truth?" Derrick asked softly. "I'm done with secrets. I've had enough of them to last me a lifetime."

She took a slow, deep breath. "I am so ashamed," she whispered. The despair in her tone spoke to him. He'd been that low before. The kinship between them was instantaneous, though the reasons for their feelings had nothing to do with each other. Confusion threaded through her voice, as well –another emotion that Derrick had known plenty of throughout his life. Leah knew this was not the answer…but what else *was* there for her?

Derrick reached out to cup her cheek in his palm. "You have no reason. This was not your fault."

When she looked up at him, her eyes glimmered with unshed tears of gratitude. "Thank you for –for saying that, but it's not how others see it."

"I don't understand," Derrick said. "I was just reminded, earlier tonight –as though I needed to be –that Cherokees are matrilineal. So your child would be considered Cherokee no matter who the father was, what matters is the mother."

"There are many," she said, "who believe there has been too much mixing with whites, that they are taking us over… and the white outlaws who come here seeking refuge from the federal lawmen are the worst. Many who would say the bastard child of one of them should not be allowed to come into our nation, and would condemn *me* for it. So much is changing with our people."

Derrick put his arm around her and after a moment, she leaned against him. Her slender shoulder relaxed into him, her fingers tightening around his hand.

"He's dead, Leah. He'll never harm you again. But you can't let him win. If you jump, it's the same as if he killed you the day he –he took advantage –"

"Who killed him?" she asked. "You?"

Derrick smiled at her eager questions. "No. Not me. A good friend of mine, Charley Blackfeather. And he didn't go easy, Leah."

"What happened? All of it –" she added quickly. "I want to know."

When Derrick had told her the entire story of Kathleen's kidnapping, his desperate attempt to free her, and of how Charley and some of the other men of Wolf Creek had come to his aid, Leah sat silent.

"Did I put you to sleep?"

She shook her head against him, giving a light chuckle. "No. It has been a very long time since I've been able to converse with anyone about this. Josie is kind, but of course…she can't understand." She sighed. "I've wished him dead so often. Thought of my sister –and her success in killing her attacker. Why couldn't I have been able to do the same?" She fell silent a moment before she went on. "Thank you for telling me, Derrick. Maybe there will be no more nightmares now." She sat up straight, looking into his eyes. "Your injuries –you recovered?"

113

"Sure."

"Strong medicine protected you."

Derrick grinned. "There's no stronger medicine than Charley Blackfeather, Leah. No better friend to have, for certain."

She shook her head. "No. I don't know this Charley Blackfeather, Derrick. But to me, *you* are the best friend to have. You convinced me not to –to do what I had planned. My cousin will tell you that when I decide on something, I rarely change my course. Yet, you managed to sway my decision."

"Twice."

"How so?"

"You're calling me *Derrick* now –not 'Mister McCain.'"

\*\*\*

"Leah!" Josie called.

Derrick turned to look behind them. Josie was rushing toward them. Reluctantly, Leah rose to her feet. "Here, Josie! I'm here."

Austen followed close behind his wife. As they neared, Josie hugged her cousin.

"I was worried about you! When you didn't come back, I –"

Leah smiled as if she thought her cousin was being silly. "You worry too much, Josie. Did anyone ever tell you that?"

"I do," Austen answered. "All the time." The teasing note in his voice lightened the moment. He turned to Derrick. "Get everything straight with your father?"

Derrick nodded. "Yes. He seems to be feeling much better now."

"And you?"

Derrick hesitated. A lot had changed for him, and even though he wasn't certain as to how everything would end, no matter what, it would be good.

His mother certainly deserved the happiness that Collin Ridge offered –the thing she'd longed for all these years but had put aside because of her children and her own uncertainty. He was glad to see her happy for once – truly happy.

Now that he'd talked face-to-face with his father, he felt at peace with himself. No matter what had happened in his life, he understood now who he was. There was no more questioning. Something else had happened, too –something he'd never planned on or considered. *Leah Martin.* There was something about her spirit that touched him as no other woman ever had.

He'd never been one to believe in destiny, but how else could the timing of her visit and his be explained? There was no denying the hot flare of desire that leapt between them, stronger with each moment they spent in one another's company; but it was more than that. The unspoken words that brought healing of their wounded spirits; the gentle touch of their hands that seemed to give one another strength; the glances that passed between them that invoked a silent understanding –all these things he'd never experienced with another –only with Leah –whom he'd met but a few hours earlier.

*Leah, who was pregnant by a man Derrick had hated down to his soul.*

115

"Derrick?" Austen asked again when Derrick didn't reply. "Everything all right?"

"Uh…yeah. I –" He broke off, shaking his head quickly. "Just…a lot of changes."

Josie gave him a questioning look that turned into one of womanly understanding. "Let's go back inside, Leah," she said quickly. "It will soon be time to put the little ones to bed." She took her cousin's arm and started for the small house, leaving Derrick awash in a current of emotion almost as violent as the swollen river swirling behind him.

Austen chuckled as Leah cast a glance backward, then squared her shoulders and marched on toward the cabin with Josie at her side.

"She's a wildcat, Leah is."

Derrick slowly turned to look at his friend.

Austen regarded him in amused silence before he continued. "You wouldn't want her, Derrick. She's not for you."

Anger surged hot inside him. "Why not, Austen? Am I too *white* for Leah's family?"

Austen shrugged, unperturbed. "That could be an issue –since it was an Anglo who raped her…an Anglo who murdered her sister, Rachel. I assume your father told you why she's here, with us. Maybe it would be easier to just let things lie."

"Don't tell me what to do."

"Advice, that's all." Austen laid a hand on Derrick's shoulder.

Derrick flung it off and moved away. "Unwanted and unasked for advice," he answered tightly.

Austen came up close behind Derrick. "What kind of father could you be to Clark Davis's baby?" he asked in a low voice. "A man who kidnapped your sister, rode with the likes of Jim Danby, tortured you –and attacked the townspeople of Wolf Creek?"

Derrick's fists clenched. "Austenaco –"

"How would you feel, knowing he'd raped the woman you love? Every time you looked at the child –"

The right cross Derrick threw as he whirled took Austen by surprise, knocking him to the ground on the rock ledge. Derrick followed him down, his fist raised again, but Austen caught it and they rolled and tumbled, trading blows, until they lay near the farthest edge of the abutment.

Derrick landed on top, looking down into Austen's dark eyes. Blood ran and dripped from his nose to the front of Austen's shirt.

"Get off me," Austen said, giving Derrick a rough shove. Amusement colored his tone. "You're bleeding on my clothes."

The sound of the rushing water escalated with the blood pounding through Derrick's veins. *What the hell was he doing?* Austen was a friend. He'd only asked the questions Derrick had asked himself earlier…it was right Austen would be interested. Leah was family.

Derrick moved slowly off of Austen, rolling onto the flat rock so that they lay side by side, both panting.

"I'm glad you didn't make me kick the shit out of you," Austen wheezed, levering himself upward into a sitting position. He held his ribs as he pushed himself upright.

Derrick gave a reluctant grin, swiping at the blood on his face. "Me, too."

Austen wiped a trickle of blood from his mouth with a grimace. "Why'd you get so damn mad?"

Derrick gave an incredulous snort of laughter as he sat up. "You know why. You just pushed too hard, Austen."

"Which part?"

"All of it." Derrick rose slowly to his feet, leaning over, hands on his knees. "Leah's not my woman. I'm not in love with her. Just met her."

Austen watched him as the silence mounted. Derrick raised his head, shouldering away a thin line of blood from his cheek.

"I think," Austen said slowly, "what made you the angriest was something else."

Derrick remained quiet. His friend was about to lay open a wound he'd tried to conceal since he'd been old enough to recognize the pain. Austen meant well, because he'd found happiness of his own –but that kind of contentment wasn't given to everyone.

"What made you angriest, Derrick, is that fact that it could all be within your reach. For once the choice can be yours –stay here, with us, or go back to Wolf Creek."

*"Choose."* Derrick chuckled wryly. "Choose my Cherokee blood –or my white blood. Give up the place in Wolf Creek, or leave here again." As he spoke, he felt as if the woods around him called to him to stay…*stay*. He had not realized how much he'd missed this place…or, maybe he had known it all along. Perhaps it was the very reason he *hadn't* come back in all these years. Now that he knew

who his real father was, there was even more reason for him to stay here. But he'd lived a lie his entire life. How could he change that now?

"What will happen to Leah?" Derrick asked hollowly.

As the careful wariness veiled Austen's eyes, Derrick knew there was a secret here.

Austen picked his words carefully. "She...will stay with us. She *is* Josie's blood."

"What of her parents? Brothers and sisters?"

Austen stood up and pulled a bandana from his pocket, dabbing at the blood on his face. "They were not so happy with the outcome of Leah's fate," he said slowly. "She was the elder of the two girls. Blame was placed on her for wandering too far –"

*"That's bullshit!* Everyone goes there to pick berries –it's one of the best places."

Austen shook his head. "Too dangerous, now, as we've learned –but there was no reason to believe that when Leah and Rachel went. Now, they've laid the blame for Rachel's death at Leah's doorstep." He sighed. "And they've convinced her it was her fault, that *she* should've been the one murdered rather than Rachel."

Derrick gave a muttered curse. "No one has seen what that gang is truly capable of. If they knew, they'd never blame her for a damn thing. She's lucky to be alive."

Austen snorted contemptuously. "Tell *her* that, Derrick." He shook his head. "I know what she was doing down here tonight," he murmured. "I'd never tell Josie, but I know. And unless she is given a reason to keep living, she –she'll find a way to end it all." He blew out a

119

long breath, meeting Derrick's eyes. "She explained everything that happened, expecting understanding...sympathy...maybe even –vengeance for Rachel's death and her own defilement."

"But she got none of that from her own family?" Derrick asked. "Why not?"

A smile touched Austen's lips. "You don't know Leah's family. Her father –well, with him, the blame always lies with another. Her mother has learned to –shall we say –*acquiesce* in all things."

Derrick shook his head. "Something I don't believe would come easy to Leah." He thought of the proud way she held herself; the defiant fire in her eyes...how could such a lovely creature destroy herself? How could a family instill that kind of self-loathing in such a beautiful spirit?

Yet...his 'father' had done it to him in other ways. Maybe he and Leah had more in common than he'd thought.

"No." Austen shook his head. "She is proud. But that's why she believes death is her only escape, now that she is ruined."

Derrick understood. *What choices did Leah have?* A family who had all but cast her out for something she'd had no control over, a younger sister's death she felt responsible for; carrying the child of her rapist, a man who had been unspeakably cruel –living must not seem like much of a choice...Leah's integrity was about to force her to do the only thing she felt left to her.

"There is...another choice, of course..." Austen murmured. "If someone asked for her hand. Someone who could accept another man's child as his own...someone who could see the beauty of Leah's spirit, and wouldn't allow it to be crushed by others. Someone who would love and protect her the way she should have always been cherished –and never was."

Derrick smiled. "If you weren't married to Josie, I'd say you'd be the perfect man for Leah."

Austen remained solemn. "But I *am* married, my friend. It is *you* who is still unattached."

Derrick's smile faded. "Matchmaking, Austen?"

The two men stood looking at one another until finally Derrick said, "What makes you think –hell, she's so damn beautiful –I just met her –she's –" He finally stopped talking, seeing the warmth of laughter in Austen's gaze.

"It is true you've only just met. And under odd circumstances. But –have you ever thought that perhaps these things happened as they were meant to?" Austen's voice was cautious, as if he understood the shock to Derrick's thoughts, to entertain such ideas. "Derrick," he pressed, "things happen for reasons we do not understand at the time –sometimes, we *never* understand. But…this chance might never come for you and Leah again."

Derrick's thoughts went to the odd twists and turns in his relationship with Charley Blackfeather, his friend – *now*. But he and Charley hadn't always been so close. They'd fought on opposite sides of the War, and Derrick had been ordered to kill Charley. Refusing, he'd been shot and left for dead himself. When Jim Danby's gang had raided Wolf Creek, he and Charley had ridden together in the posse that had gone after the outlaws. It was during that time they'd grudgingly become friends. In the months

121

since then, that friendship had grown, strengthening to brotherhood, dependability and trust –things that didn't come easy to either of them.

"You've been alone too long."

"That's my business," Derrick answered sharply.

Austen shrugged. "Can you say you're truly happy? No…I didn't think so. That's why you got so mad. You *know* what I'm saying is the truth."

Derrick kept his face impassive. Was he that transparent?

As if Austen had heard Derrick's thoughts, he smiled. "Leah would have you if you asked. It wouldn't be easy. She has her pride. But, it seems, so do you. I don't know if it would ever happen –two prideful souls such as yourselves –you might ignore the happiness you could have together."

"I take it you and Josie have nothing but happy days?" Derrick asked caustically.

Austen chuckled. "Far from it, my friend. But that's part of life. I thought I couldn't love her any stronger than I did when we said the wedding words. But as the years have passed, and with the things we've shared –good and bad –I love her more than ever."

"That's fine for you, but –"

"Think about it, brother." Austen stepped forward, clapping Derrick's shoulder. "We'd better get back. They'll be coming down here to check on us. Let's wash this blood off." He stood looking into Derrick's eyes. "No matter what, I'm glad you discovered what Leah was about to do tonight. You saved her life –this time."

\*\*\*

122

As they walked back up the embankment of the river bed, Austen caught his breath, swearing as he came to a stop. "That looks like David Martin's horse."

"Leah's father? What's he doing here?"

There were three horses tethered at the front of the little cabin. Austen peered at them, then said, "I don't know those other two –"

The wariness in Austen's voice made Derrick give him a sharp look. "Think there could be trouble of some kind?"

"Maybe. I have no use for Martin."

"Let's go see."

Raised voices filtered from inside the cabin as they neared.

Austen put a staying hand on Derrick's arm. "Just wait. Let's see what we're walking into."

"Leah, you will return! As my daughter, you will do as I say," Martin announced.

"Why?" Derrick breathed, shooting Austen a quick glance. They stood just below the open window of the front room, out of sight.

Austen shook his head, but Derrick could read the knowledge in his friend's eyes, even before Martin spoke again.

"John Red Bird has offered for your hand."

"*Jesus!*" Derrick started out from the shadows. He didn't know David Martin, but he sure as *hell* knew John Red Bird. Or, knew *of* him. His reputation for cruelty bordered on insanity. There was no way her father could be unaware of that fact.

"I won't –" Leah began from inside, but whatever she was about to say was cut off as Derrick threw the door open and stepped inside.

Leah looked up at him, humiliation staining the tawny loveliness of her skin. In her eyes, though, he could see she was not going to give in and go quietly with her father.

The idea that Martin had not succeeded in crushing his daughter's spirit all these years was something Derrick could not put aside. He knew her thoughts of ending her life were not because of the disfavor she'd fallen into with her father. Nor were they for her *own* dishonor. She had been thinking of the child –a child she had not wanted, yet, somehow, had come to love, despite the brutal circumstances of its very existence. And regardless of who the father had been. No matter what, it was half hers –and she wanted to protect it from life without a father.

Half-white, fitting into neither world, Leah's son or daughter would be plummeted into the loneliest existence imaginable. And how would Leah be able to fend for both of them?

"Things were getting loud in here," Austen said in soft warning, looking around the room.

"I'm here to take Leah home as my wife." John Red Bird spoke as if it were fact already and there was no need for her agreement.

"I wouldn't marry you if you begged me!"

Red Bird turned to face her, his lips turning upward into a snarl. "It is *you* who will be begging! I am humiliating myself by taking you to wife. If your father wasn't giving me so many horses, I would leave you here to rot –you and your bastard."

The last word had barely left his mouth before Derrick was upon him, leaping past Leah as she took a startled step backward. He tackled Red Bird to the floor of the small cabin.

Derrick raised his fist and slammed it into Red Bird's nose, feeling a satisfying crunch. But Red Bird recovered from his surprise as anger took over. He rolled, pinning Derrick under him, taking a savage swing at Derrick.

Derrick caught his arm, looking up into the murderous face above him. *How could any father allow his daughter to be betrothed to such a man?*

He managed to push Red Bird off, and both of them grappled for a good hold on one another as they rose to their knees, then stood.

Red Bird reached to pull a blade from his belt, and Derrick heard Leah's gasp from behind him.

Red Bird's move didn't put fear in Derrick's heart, by any means. The things he'd been through in his past made this fight seem like child's play. Red Bird was predictable. When he lunged, Derrick seized his arm with both hands, bringing it down on the edge of the table. Red Bird's wrist snapped like a dry tree branch. He cried out, giving a high-pitched scream, then fell on the floor, cradling his broken wrist.

Derrick stood over him, panting. "Listen to me," he said, watching Red Bird writhe on the floor. "Both of you." He shot Martin a hard look. "Leah will *not* be forced to marry against her will."

Martin started forward, and Austen gripped his shoulder with a firm hand. He stopped, pinning Derrick with a baleful glare. "You have made a mistake," he declared. "My daughter will do as I say until she is married. And I say she *will* marry John Red Bird." He cast a look at Leah. "What are you waiting for? Go and gather your things."

But Leah raised her head proudly, refusing to move. When Derrick turned to look at her, she did not meet his eyes, but looked through her father as if he were made of glass. Tears welled in her eyes, and she held herself stiffly.

The room was silent but for Red Bird's mewling and gasping for breath on the floor at Derrick's feet. Red Bird must have gotten in a couple of good punches, he thought, his hand going to his bruised ribs. Or maybe that soreness was courtesy of his earlier fight with Austen. That brought a fleeting smile to his lips.

Remembering what had brought this battle with John Red Bird about, his earlier anger returned quickly.

Derrick had only been in love once in his life, with a woman who had betrayed him. While he'd been away fighting for the Confederacy, Jolene had married a Union soldier. She had been a beautiful woman, but Derrick had never been certain of her —as it turned out, with good cause.

Looking at the defiance in Leah's lovely features, he knew he could always be sure of her, no matter what. She had an honesty that both heartened and amused him; and a sweet sincerity that could be the forerunner of love.

Did she see any redeeming quality in him, he wondered? No matter what he'd done, he didn't believe she would reject him over John Red Bird. He hadn't given marriage another thought after Jolene had done what she'd done. Leah was a lady. She needed someone to be kind to her, to provide for her; someone to make a home with for her little one –and others that might follow.

"Think about it," Austen had said. But how could he? How could *she*?

Much as she might want to believe she had a choice –Derrick and she both knew what it had narrowly escaped being earlier this evening. There was no more time to "think about it." He met Leah's eyes.

"Leah and I are going to be married," he heard himself saying. "And Martin, you can keep your damn horses."

\*\*\*

Martin and Red Bird stomped from the cabin, headed for the medicine man's quarters to get Red Bird's arm set before they started for home.

"You are dead to me," Martin told Leah as he started out the door.

"As you are to me," she replied haughtily.

Martin looked as if he'd like to give her a slap for her insolence, but Derrick stepped forward, putting himself between them.

The door slammed shut, and Josie gathered the children, shooing them into their beds.

"A wise decision," Austen said softly to Derrick. "I leave you two to sort out your plans." With a wink, he turned to follow Josie to the bedroom.

It was Leah who came to Derrick and took his hand in hers.

"Are you sorry you spoke for me?" She looked up at him with a half-teasing light in her eyes.

He gave a short laugh. "No. Are *you*?"

She shook her head. "It's late. Maybe you'd rather sleep…think about it…I won't hold you to it in the morning, if you've changed your mind."

He moved to put his arms around her. "That's enough 'thinking about it'. I'm not gonna change my mind."

She laughed softly.

"What's funny?" he asked.

"What we were talking about earlier, about how, in our society, our standing comes from our mothers' side. Women have much power in our culture," she teased. The smile faded and she became serious again. "I wondered…has it occurred to you that –no matter *who* your father is, or is not –if you marry me, you will be officially a Cherokee citizen? And…our children will always know their heritage. "

"They'll never have to wonder, no doubt about that." He gave her a wry smile. "Once we're married, there'll be no turning back, Leah –for either of us."

"Derrick, there's something I have to know –"

"I already suspect what it is you're worried about. It's not about you and me. We're gonna be fine. Love – that'll come with time, with a good start. It's the baby…about it being Clark Davis's baby, and about him raping you."

Leah laid her head on Derrick's shoulder and he could feel the warmth of her tears on his shirt.

"Can you love him, or her? Can you be a good father? My father was a tyrant –"

Derrick gave a faint smile at the understatement. "Yet, look at you." He held her away from him, staring down into her face. "You survived, and you're so –" he broke off, fumbling for the right words.

"Stubborn?" she supplied. "Stiff-necked?"

"No." He ran his thumb over the soft silk of her hair, pulled back into a loose bun. "So damn beautiful – inside and out."

Tears sprang to her eyes. "It almost sounds as if you mean those pretty words."

"I do, Leah. If I could've done this any differently, I would've. Given us some time…made a better impression on your father." He grinned, and she gave a soft chuckle.

"Not that *that* would make a difference," she noted.

"Clark Davis is dead. He'll never hurt you again. And this child –" he laid a hand gently on her stomach – "doesn't know a thing about how he's gotten here or what kind of person his father was. I think…if we try…we can keep it that way until he's old enough to understand."

"You fought for me…for *us* –" She placed her hand atop his. "Derrick, no one's ever done that before. No one has ever…" She moved to touch his cheek.

In that moment, Derrick knew he would always fight for her, and for her child, no matter what. He'd drifted long enough; seen enough of the seedy side of the world. He was ready for something good in his life. He

129

wasn't the only one who had suffered, but one thing he knew –he wasn't alone anymore. When it had happened, he wasn't sure –maybe when he'd come upon Leah pondering her jump from the rock shelf earlier tonight. Maybe even earlier, when she'd questioned him at the table.

He'd always tried to do the right thing –but he'd gotten sidetracked. Still, the desire was there to be the kind of man he knew he could be, but had given up on. Raising Clark Davis's child would be a challenge. But he'd seen the love and protectiveness for her child in Leah's face earlier when her father and John Red Bird had crowded the doorway of the small cabin. Even her thoughts of ending her life had been to protect the baby.

His father's words came back to him, as if whispered on the still, autumn night.

"It takes a man to raise another man's son," Derrick said softly, "with kindness in his heart, no matter the circumstances."

Leah's beautiful dark eyes grew misty, as if he was giving her a dream she could never have imagined, or asked for. Someday, he would tell her everything about his own upbringing. Someday, he'd tell her how deeply he understood *exactly* what he was committing himself to. But for now, he only pulled her close and put a finger to her lips as she started to speak. No one else could understand what Leah was feeling right now –no one but him. The words were simple –a promise he could make her as no other man in the world could. Trust and love had to start somewhere.

"I am that man, Leah." And then, so there would be no misunderstanding that he intended to embrace both the white world and his Cherokee side that had been so long denied, he said it again as she came into his arms. In Cherokee. In her language –in *their* language.

And with everything in him, he meant it.

### THE END

## ASA PEPPER'S PLACE
### By
### Jerry Guin

Deputy Marshal Quint Croy was making his late evening rounds. It was a clear, bright, moonlit night, with a light breeze from the north. Things seemed to be quiet on Quint's assigned route, the streets of lower Wolf Creek – the area known as Dogleg City. Usually, by this time of night, he would have been called upon to quell some sort of disturbance at one of the drinking and gambling establishments, hopefully before it turned into gunplay.

The drovers that had brought herds of longhorns from Texas expected cheap liquor, a winning hand at cards, and maybe some female companionship when they entered this section of town. Many had started their quest for booze and friendly faces on the higher side, or north end, of town, then instinctively moved on. Perhaps a smiling dealer had raked in three days of their pay in one turn of the cards, or one of the painted floozies had promised euphoria for a lofty token. The higher-than-usual prices sent many in search of a more affordable atmosphere.

It was the middle of the week, not that a mid-week night was any different than a weekend night when cattle drovers were in town. The nighttime activities of the patrons of Dogleg City, where the lowest class establishments were found, were anything but quiet. Yellow light, a cloud of blue tobacco smoke, a woman's loud –and probably fraudulent –laughter, and the usual

132

crowd reverie greeted Quint as he peered over the bat-wing doors of the Lucky Break Saloon. The Lucky Break was the largest, brightest establishment in this part of town. It was located on the northern boundary of Dogleg City, at the corner of Second and Ulysses S. Grant Streets. Gambling was the mainstay of The Lucky Break, with liquor readily available and a two-dollar woman at one's calling. Quint looked around the crowded room, but did not detect anything out of the ordinary. He walked to the middle of the street, so as to have a full view of the business fronts. He stepped aside as two mounted cowboys walked their horses past him –there were no boardwalks fronting the buildings in this part of town. He was watchful and wary, with his right hand lodged on the butt of his holstered six-gun. He knew from experience that a violent outbreak could occur at any time. Quint watched as the two mounted men guided their horses, a block away, to a hitch-rail at the front of Asa's Saloon.

Quint headed on down Second Street to check out the usually quiet Red Chamber, a Chinese-owned opium den, which was across the street from the potentially explosive Asa's Saloon. Asa Pepper's place was known to be the toughest place in all of Wolf Creek. The saloon was housed in a dilapidated, rectangular wood-frame building made of rough board siding that had weathered gray. The hitch-rails were located close to the front wall of the building. Inside, the wares were purveyed by the light of candles or lanterns –which were dim, at best.

There were no prejudices behind the bar at Asa's Saloon. Anyone with the price could get a drink, a game of cards or a whore for half the cost of the establishments on the north end of town. Asa's was a haven for buffalo hunters, prairie wolfers, Celestials, Mexicans and blacks from Matthias, the all black town twenty miles to the east. Once in awhile a half-breed Indian or two would show up. Those on the dodge from the law often frequented the place, as well, but rarely caused disturbances that would bring attention to themselves. Occasionally, a trooper or two came in from nearby Fort Braxton. The soldiers never stayed long, for they were usually near-broke when they rode in –hoping for a sponsored drink or two before their awaited payday, which was fifty cents a day, less than half as much as a working cowboy.

After Asa's grand opening, the business had begun to grow daily as word got around of the saloon's cheaper prices. When the whiskey drummers had gotten wind of the new establishment, they had fallen over themselves getting to Asa's to convince him to stock their product – they soon learned that Asa would stock only the cheapest brands, but that he paid. Nor was Asa above offering his own homemade creek water whiskey to customers who knew that he had previously dealt in the stuff at Matthias. The usual price of twenty-five cents for half-a-glass was a lot cheaper than bottled whiskey. Sorghum beer was also a mainstay, and Asa made money on it even at a nickel a glass.

Asa usually did all the bartending, though a friend from Matthias, Harry Turner, helped out from time to time. Asa once told Quint that it was Harry who had talked Asa into allowing him to introduce a few soiled doves as a separate business. He wanted to bring in two young women from Matthias, a black girl and an Indian girl, as well as two older cast-offs from The Wolf's Den.

"It'll be good for business," Harry had said. "The men will buy drinks for themselves, and for the women, too." Asa liked Harry and wanted to see him make a few bucks, so he had agreed to the deal –as long as the women did their drinking in the saloon, and their other business in the cribs out back. Servicing their customers in plain sight would not have been tolerated even in Dogleg City –plus, it would inevitably lead to fights, and there were already enough of those to go around.

Quint could hear the boisterous laughter before he got within thirty feet of the entrance. Suddenly, a loud voice from within the walls yelled, "You black son of a bitch, I'm gonna kill you!"

Quint quickened to a run, while drawing his .44 caliber cap-and-ball Army Colt. Quint burst through the entrance to the saloon, and raked his eyes around the crowded room. A scattering of tables on the right-hand side were full of card players and loungers. On the left, at the far end of the bar, six men stood idle and wide-eyed. All eyes were directed to Asa Pepper, who was bent back against the bar, wedged there by a tall man in cowboy garb. The front of Asa's shirt was slashed open and covered in blood. The man was pushing Asa's chin back with his left hand, and brandished a long-bladed knife in his right. Asa's right hand clawed the fingers at his throat, and his left gripped the knife-wielder's right wrist, desperately holding the blade away.

Another tall cowboy stood nearby, a six-gun in one hand, apparently covering the action. When Quint

135

advanced, the man with the six-gun swung the weapon around without hesitation, and fired a shot. The revolver boomed out, rocking the interior of the saloon with its thunder. The shot mule-kicked Quint's upper left arm –he was forced back a step from its impact. The deputy squeezed the trigger of his .44, sending a bullet that punched a hole in the gunman's shirt front. The cowboy was stunned by the jolt of the bullet hitting him; he blinked his eyes, then fumbled in an attempt to cock his single action six-gun. Quint side-stepped out of the thick, gray cloud of his-own gun-smoke and fired again. This bullet hit the man in the upper chest. This time, the cowboy pitched forward onto the floor, rolled and lay still.

At the same time, Asa brought a knee up sharply into his attacker's groin. The action caused the man to loosen his grip on the bar-owner's throat. Asa slipped around, punched the cowboy twice in the belly, then shoved him onto the floor. He gave the man a kick to the ribs then jumped on top of him. Now face-to-face, Asa wrestled the knife away. Then he raised himself up at the hips and thrust the knife into the man's chest. Asa pulled the knife free, then raised it above his head –preparing to stab again.

Though wounded himself, Quint quickly stepped forward and swiped the barrel of his Colt to the back of Asa's head before he could thrust the blade again. Asa Pepper dropped the knife and fell sideways. Quint retrieved the knife and the cowboy's holstered six-gun. The barely-conscious man moaned. Quint stepped over and checked the motionless man he had shot twice. He then checked his own arm wound. The numbness had started to fade, and it was throbbing with each beat of his heart. The wound was high up –fortunately the bullet had passed through without hitting any bones. He stuffed a bandana over the entrance hole while a patron, a short man in a derby hat, stepped forward and pressed his own handkerchief against the exit wound, "It ain't bleeding much, deputy," he said.

Asa, who had been out briefly, began to stir. He blinked, winced from the pain, then held a hand to his head and sat up.

"I guess you had no choice but to hit me, deputy. I would have killed him. He's crazy drunk –he would have cut me up if I hadn't stopped him."

Quint stood over the downed trio, then looked around the room. He saw a familiar face, and called out, "Harry, send someone to get Doc Munro. These men are in bad shape. And I don't feel so good myself."

He turned to Asa, "What happened here?"

Asa shrugged his shoulder, "It's like I said, he's crazy drunk."

"Do you know him?" Quint asked.

Asa stood. He was still breathing hard. He looked around. "He came in while I was clearing one of the tables. He would of never got ahold of me if I was behind the bar, I got an axe handle and a loaded shotgun back there. And I left my Walker Colt back there instead of stickin' it in my belt, like a dern fool."

"I asked if you know him," Quint said. "I want to know why he attacked you."

Asa straightened up, then set the glassware on the bar, "I knew him from a time ago. Let me see to business Quint, and I'll tell you all about it."

"No deal, Asa. Somebody else can see to the business. There's one man dead, and you were trying to kill the other one. I want some answers right now, before Marshal Gardner hears about this. He'll be mad as hell, and want to close you down."

Asa nodded. He knew the marshal was none too fond of him.

"When the doctor is finished here," Quint said, "I'm going to take this fella to jail, if he's still alive. You're going to join him in a cell if you don't come clean."

"All right, Quint. Harry can watch the place while I'm gone."

Quint turned and faced the other patrons, who were uncharacteristically quiet.

"Anyone know these two?" No one in the room responded, other than to shake their heads.

When Doc Munro arrived, he looked at Quint's wound first. He checked the entrance and exit wounds briefly, then said, "It's not too bad, Quint. I'll check the others, then I'll clean you up. You need to sit down, though, you're looking a little ashen."

Quint took a nearby chair. The doctor confirmed that the gunman lying on his stomach was dead. The man that Asa had stabbed was unconscious. Doctor Munro applied a heavy compress to the wound and bandaged it in place.

"We don't want any nasty sucking wounds, do we," he said, mostly to himself.

Then he placed his left hand on the man's chest, tapping the middle finger of that hand with his right middle finger.

Doctor Munro stood. "I don't know what internal damage was done, time will tell. The wound seems deep, and there's no immediate evidence of a collapsed lung, but I won't be able to tell without a closer examination. Here, a couple of you men carry him to my buggy out front."

No one moved. The doc's face darkened.

"I said pick him up, damn it," he said. "Or I'll bloody well remember it when it's one of you bleeding in this hellhole."

Two customers quickly stepped forward and obeyed.

The doctor then returned his attention to Quint. He washed Quint's wounds, then bandaged them.

"I'll stitch you up in a bit, when I've seen to everyone. You might want to sling that arm for a few days, otherwise just keep the wounds clean. Come and see me in two days, I want to make sure there's no mortification."

Doctor Munro washed and bandaged Asa's slashed chest wound, and said, "You're lucky it was no deeper. It's a flesh wound; just keep it clean and change the bandage daily." He examined the spot where Quint's gun barrel had connected with Asa's scalp, and dabbed it with alcohol. "A cold compress on that might keep the swelling down."

When Doctor Munro was finished, he said, "My buggy is out front. If you like, Quint, I can drop you and your prisoner off at the jail and tend to him further there.

I'll let Elijah Gravely know to pick up the deceased man and take him to the funeral home."

Quint nodded, then looked over at Asa. "You'd better come along, too," he said, and the barman stood to comply.

Asa turned to one of the girls. "Go fetch Harry," he said. "Tell him I'll be back directly."

Quint climbed into the front of the buggy, beside Doc Munro. Asa sat in the back, beside the supine form of the man who had tried to kill him.

***

While the buggy rolled down the dark streets on its way to the county jail, Asa Pepper's mind wandered, reliving the events that had brought him to this point.

The former slave had come to Wolf Creek almost a year earlier. Not long after his arrival, he had found himself in an office chair at the bank, awaiting an answer to his proposal of buying a deserted building. He'd spoken at length about the place with a suited bank employee named Allen Cook. Cook's interest was keen because the building was in a poor, rather blighted location –any opportunity to sell it would be very welcome.

Since Asa did not offer the full purchase price in cash, Cook asked about his ability to pay a mortgage if allowed to make monthly payments.

"I plan to make it into a saloon," Asa had answered. "Way I hear it, this new railroad coming through will be bringing in more cowboys than you can shake a stick at, all thirsty from driving their herds here. Money won't be a problem, once things get going."

"As I understand it," Cook said, "you *could* pay cash for the building, but you need what cash you have in order to buy products for the business?"

Asa nodded,

Cook stood. "I'll talk to the bank manager."

He disappeared into a back office to confer with the manager, Melvin Lohorn. It was several minutes before he returned and sat back down.

"Mr. Lohorn agreed to accept your one-hundred-dollar down payment on the three hundred dollar price, with a payment of thirty dollars due on the first of each month. He stressed that –the *first*, not the second. I have the papers for you to sign. Or mark."

"What's the interest rate?" Asa asked.

"Eight percent."

"That's kind of steep."

Cook shrugged. "Believe me, it took some convincing to talk him into that. The letter you brought made all the difference –the Crown W is the biggest ranch in these parts, and a good word from its foreman goes a long way. Jake Andrews is honest as the day is long –and his boss, old man Sparkman, is cantankerous as, well, as a man can be. No one wants to get crossways of him, that's for sure. If not for that, we'd most likely not be offering you any loan at all."

Asa leaned forward and smiled –but not with his eyes.

"Did you tell Mr. Lohorn what color I am?"

Cook paused. "Well, that may have slipped my mind. But no one really wants that old place, and I want to get what we can out of it while we have a chance. So for

141

goodness sake, make your mark and leave before he comes out of his office."

Asa signed his full name and passed the paper back to Cook.

Asa Pepper, who'd spent more than five decades a slave, walked out of the bank that day a businessman and property owner. He had found his place in the world.

*\*\*\**

They arrived at the jail, which was attached to the sheriff's office. Quint and Asa, injured though they both were, gamely attempted to help Doc Munro carry the unconscious cowboy from the back of the buggy to the jail –fortunately, the deputy on duty, young Zack Zacherly, came outside and relieved them of their share of the burden. They lodged the prisoner on a cot inside a cell, and the doctor began to work once more on his injuries.

Quint started to walk away –Dr. Munro called out to him without looking up.

"You're not going anywhere, deputy, until I stitch you up. I'll be finished here in a moment, at least for now."

After the doctor's ministrations on him were complete, Quint ushered Asa to the front door.

"Walk over to the marshal's office with me," Quint said. "And let's talk."

They left Sheriff Satterlee's jail and made the one-block journey to Marshal Gardner's office, which was empty –the Marshal was making his own rounds.

He motioned Asa to sit in a ladder-backed chair. Quint wet a towel for Asa's head, now swollen from the blow the deputy had given him.

"Hold this cloth on your head Asa," he said. Asa reached up and held the towel in place.

Quint took a seat behind his desk, "Any time you're ready."

Asa removed the towel and lay it on the desk, then sighed and began to talk.

"His name is Watson Brown," Asa announced. "Everybody called him Watty. Some four, five years ago, me and him both worked for the Circle T ranch, over near Sweetwater, on the Brazos, down in Texas. He's a cattle drover. My wife Ruby did the cooking for the ranch hands, while I took care of the buildings and growings."

Quint looked surprised. "I didn't know you came from Texas, Asa. I guess I figured that you'd come from somewhere deep in the south."

Asa smiled. "Everybody's from someplace or another. I was born in Tennessee, not far from Memphis. My momma and daddy were both slaves when I was born. A man by the name of Simon Thatcher owned us. He never really treated us bad, not the way some white folks did. He let me marry a woman he owned. Ruby and I never stood before no preacher or nothing, we just lived together, but before long everybody knew we was married. That's how it was for folks like us. Sometimes Simon would give us a little money we could spend in town for clothes and tobacco and candy. I liked the old man, he had a good heart. It wasn't a bad life –it was just life, we made the most we could of it."

"You don't talk like an ignorant former slave, Asa," Quint said. "Fact is, every other time I've heard you

143

speak before, especially when Marshal Gardner is near, you sounded like you were fresh out of the cotton fields."

Asa nodded. "Marshal Gardner thinks all black people are ignorant, so I just give him what he expects. Missus Thatcher taught me to read. She insisted that all of us learn to read and cipher. She said we'd get along better if we were educated."

Quint nodded. "That was damned decent of her."

"It sure was," Asa said, "especially since it was against the law."

"Go on," Quint said.

Asa took a breath, "Simon and Missus Thatcher had themselves a son, Jonas. He was a fine young man. He grew up quick, and acted a lot like his daddy. When Jonas was about twenty-five he got itchy feet. He said he was tired of farming and wanted a more exciting life, so one day he took off and went to Texas. About six months later, Missus Thatcher took sick and died. When Jonas had come back he started talking to the old man about selling out and moving to Texas to raise cattle. Simon would not have any of it; he was not about to sell and leave the family home where his wife was buried. Jonas argued some, but nothing came of it. After awhile Jonas left, and we didn't see him again until four years later when Simon up and died from some fever. Word got to Jonas and he came home right away. Within the year, Jonas gathered me and Ruby, and two others, together and talked to us.

"I've sold the place," he said. "We'll be moving to Texas come Monday morning."

We left, just like he said. We had everything packed into eight wagons. Me and Jimbo drove along what cattle Jonas had, thirty head or so, including two milk cows. Jonas sold all the chickens and hogs. It took us near a month to get to where Jonas had bought a ranch in Texas that he named the Circle T.

"It didn't take long before we were settled in. We'd never been any place further than twenty miles from home before. Ruby and I were both homesick, but Jonas told us that we should forget the old place and make a good life right there. He said things were changing and that there could be a war coming; that it wasn't safe for us in Tennessee any longer. It turned out that he was right – about moving, and about the war. They say that the Union Army stripped and burned the old home place so there's nothing left there now but memories anyway.

"Jonas had about ten cowboys he hired to take care of the cattle. There must have been three or four thousand cows there. He never had me do any of the cattle work. He said I was too old –that there was plenty of work for me to do maintaining the buildings, hay fields and gardens. And that's what I did, same work as always, while Ruby did house chores and cooking.

"One day Jonas called me and Ruby and the other two slaves to his front porch. He said the war was over and we were now freed; Mr. Lincoln had signed it into law. Jonas told us that we were free to leave, that we could go away if we wanted to. It was a shock to all of us.

"Jonas said that he'd like us to stay, that we were like part of his family, but that he would understand if we chose to leave. He said that if we stayed here, he would pay us for the work we did every day. The others thanked him for the consideration, but wanted to go out and make their own way. Ruby and I chose to stay. At the end of every month Jonas would come by and give us each an envelope with money in it, just like he paid the ranch hands.

"Everything was fine for a time, until the spring of 'sixty-seven. That's when Jonas made a deal to take a herd up to Abilene, Kansas, and sell it. He hired a bunch more cowboys to handle the herd, and bought a big string of horses.

"The night before they were to leave on the drive, everyone wanted to get to bed so's they could get an early start. That's everybody 'ceptin Watty and another man named Burl Stimson. Jonas Thatcher told all the hands to stay out of town and get rested. He wanted to get started early without a problem. Watty and Burl were both young and head strong, though, and sometimes stupid. They didn't listen. They waited until dark, then snuck off and got juiced up. That would have been fine –they're the ones that would be sick come morning. Except they didn't want the party to stop. Ruby and I were asleep in the little shanty house Mr. Thatcher built for us; it was a ways back from the main house. Those two drunks woke us up. Burl was a nasty bastard –even in daylight hours he was always pulling pranks that got others hurt, and he just laughed when something bad happened to anyone. When he got to drinking, he was mean as a bear, ready to whup ass on anyone that got in his way, or just for the fun of it.

"Watty wasn't like that until he started running with Burl. Usually Watty wouldn't do anything more than stand by, egging Burl on to some mischief. But that night was different –they were both crazy drunk.

146

"They woke us up banging on the door. Burl was giggling and laughing,

"'Open up in there! Come on out! I want me a black woman, I ain't never had one! We're coming in!'"

"Watty made the mistake of pushing through the door first. I hit him with the stove poker, stuck the curved end in his jaw. Burl was right behind him. He swung a big fist that hit me on the side of the head. It was enough to put me out.

"When I woke up, Ruby was dabbing a wet cloth to my head. She told me what had happened while I was out. Watty was out of his head, being drunk and full of pain after having the poker stuck in his jaw. He had wrenched it free and dropped it on the floor, then ran outside. Burl had gotten ahold of her and was intent on having his way with her. Her screaming and the commotion had woke up everybody. Burl was on top of her when Jonas and two others came in. She said that Jonas commenced to beat Burl senseless with that same stove poker that I had used to down Watty with. He swung one time too many, and cracked Burl's head open.

"Watty had gotten on his horse and pulled his six-gun, then started shooting when Jonas and the others went through the door. A bullet hit one of the drovers, Fred Wilson, and killed him. Watty managed to ride away. We buried Fred and Burl come daylight. I volunteered to dig the graves. I'd of killed Burl myself –him and Watty, too, if I'd had the chance. Jonas delayed the drive a few days while he and the others looked for Watty, but he was long gone. Jonas went to the sheriff and a wanted poster was put out for Watty, for killing Fred Wilson.

147

"Jonas had hired a fella to do the cooking on the drive, but after what happened he let that man go and said that he wanted me and Ruby to go along and do the cooking. I know he did it to protect us in case Watty came back to even things up.

"It was a big camp. We had near twenty men to feed three times a day. I'm not sure that first cook could have handled it by himself anyway. Jonas may have said something to the others, but not a one of them ever mentioned anything about Burl and Watty the whole trip. They were real good boys, real respectful to Ruby –and me too. When we got to Abilene in July, Jonas paid everyone off, including Ruby and me. He gave each of us a hundred dollars for wages, then handed me two more hundred dollar bills besides."

"'I want you and Ruby to stay in Kansas,' he said. 'Kansas was a free state even during the war, and I think there's more opportunity for you folks here than there is back in Texas.'

"I'll always believe that he felt that there might be some sort of reprisal for Burl Stimson's death if we were to go back.

"Before Jonas left he told me that he knew a man named Jake Andrews, that was the foreman for the Crown W Ranch, near Wolf Creek. He said for me to look up Andrews and tell him that I had been working for Jonas Thatcher. He gave me a paper that said I was a good man and looking for a new start. Ruby and I left Abilene and went to see Mr. Andrews.

"Jake Andrews was a friendly man, and he smiled when he read the note from Jonas –'I wish I could have

148

seen Jonas while he was in Kansas, he's a good man. You come highly recommended Asa, but right now I'll tell you the truth –we don't have a need for you and your wife here on the ranch. If I were you, I'd go over to Matthias. It's a settlement within a day's ride of here –all made up of colored folks from Back East, Exodusters they call themselves. Maybe there'd be an opportunity for you folks over there. It's a growing place. You're welcome to spend the night here, though. Anyone that's a friend of Jonas Thatcher is a friend of mine. We did some droving together down on the Brazos a few years ago.'

"Before we left the next morning, Jake Andrews told me, 'If you ever need anything, I want you to come back and see me.'

"He seemed sincere. He even shook my hand."

"So that's how you got to Matthias, and eventually to Wolf Creek?" Quint asked.

Asa nodded, "We went to Matthias, that's where everyone kept telling us to go. I have a place there. I go home to see Ruby once a week, the rest of the time I sleep in a back room at the saloon. I don't want her down here, it's too rough a place. I was doing a little whiskey selling and gambling from our place in Matthias, until the Sheriff shut me down one day. He said I needed to quit selling that whiskey that everyone was making and selling to the Indians. It was nothing more than grain alcohol and river water with red peppers and a twist of tobacco thrown in every barrel. It was fiery stuff, and it would sure as hell get 'em plenty drunk, though. Sheriff Satterlee was pretty decent about it, even told me about a place that was for sale. He said that if I wanted to be in business then I'd

have to do it legal-like. I went to see Jake Andrews to ask
if he would put in a word for me so that I could buy or rent
that old building. He gave me a paper to give to the
banker.

"So I came down and bought the place. *My* place. I
didn't have much money, but I was able to start in
business right away. I hadn't seen nor heard anything
about Watty Brown since that night down in Texas. I think
he was as surprised at seeing me as I was him when he
came in tonight."

Quint nodded, "Well, he wasn't alone tonight. I
take it you don't know the other man, the one that I shot?"

Asa shook his head, "No, I don't know who the
other fella was. I've never seen him before tonight."

Quint nodded. "Well, he was Watty's sidekick –
most likely the two had struck up a friendship on a trail
drive, and were in town because the cattle drive is done.
That fella may be innocent of any other wrong-doing –but
anytime someone starts shooting at the law, just because
he sees a badge, he's likely to have a bad day. Or his last
day."

"If I was to get another chance, I'd kill Watty
Brown for his part in bothering Ruby, and for him killing
Fred Wilson," Asa said.

Quint flashed a hard look at Asa, "I don't think you
want to do that Asa. That skunk's not worth getting
hanged over. That's why I hit you back there. It would be
better for you and your wife to let the law handle it. Now,
do you know what county the Circle T ranch, and this
town of Sweetwater, is in?"

Asa thought for a moment, "I believe it is Nolan County."

Quint wrote on a note pad, then said, "The law in Kansas is as good as the law in Texas. If it's like you say, that Watty Brown is wanted for murder down there, and if he lives through that stab wound he'll be taken back to answer the charges."

"Then what?"

"I'd say a Nolan County judge will see him hanged."

Asa grunted. "I hope so."

"Meanwhile," Quint said, "Marshal Gardner is not going to be happy to hear about another killing at your saloon."

Asa shook his head, "Marshal Gardner don't like me much. He treats me like I was still a slave. Sometimes I think he's just waiting for a reason to shut me down. I expect this business with Watty Brown is reason enough."

"Marshal Gardner doesn't have anything against you personally, Asa. He's just tired of all the violence around your saloon of a night. Fact is, he's been taking some heat for it lately, and it's got him on edge."

Asa was quick to answer. "If that's so, he's been on edge ever since I met him. And besides, I got no control over what a man does when he's drinking."

Quint nodded. "Marshal Gardner knows that." He stared at Asa for a moment, then added, "The Marshal is a logical man, and I don't believe that he wants Asa's Saloon to close. He told me once that as long as your saloon is open, then most of the violence is corralled in

Dogleg City instead of the establishments uptown. Do you understand what I'm saying, Asa?"

Asa got a distant look in his eye then nodded, "I think so, deputy. Some life in this town is cheaper than others, I guess. But I appreciate you trying to help."

Quint smiled. "Once I explain things to the Marshal, and we get confirmation from the Nolan County Sheriff as to the warrant on Watson Brown, I believe things will work out."

"So I can go back to work?"

"Sure," Quint said. "And maybe one day this week we can go fishing again."

Quint watched the older man trudge back to Dogleg City, then put a pot of coffee on. There was no telling what the rest of the night might bring.

THE END

## MULE-SKINNERS: JUDGE NOT
By
Jacquie Rogers

*Summer, 1871 –just east of Wolf Creek, Kansas*

(Note: this story takes place during the events of *Wolf Creek 1: Bloody Trail.*)

My pa wanted to see the Pacific Ocean. He'd flapped his lips all the way from Missouri to the middle of Kansas, and I reckoned by the time we did get to the ocean, I'd be ready to dunk him in it.

"One of the mules is lagging."

"Hermes," I hollered. "Quit sniffing that bush and get over here." Sure, my mules were coddled, but they'd been my only company for a year during the war, and the six years since, my best friends. "You know you're supposed to stay by the wagon."

The mule sent me a guilty look and trotted to his spot by the rear wheel with the other three. I have eight mules, but a harness for only four, so four mules pulled half a day, then I traded them out.

"Wouldn't it be easier to tie the spare mules to the wagon, Elsie?" My father, Obadiah Parry, had lost his wife, son, home, and thought he'd lost me and the mules in the war, but he'd run into me a few years back.

Believe me, the moment I saw that man was the happiest day of my life. His brown hair had grayed and he'd hunched over and slowed down considerable, but his

153

blue eyes still had that sparkle –the one that let you know there very well could be a frog in the sugar bowl, so watch out. I wouldn't call him a moocher, but he did let me do the working while he did the talking.

"Maybe, but I ain't tying them up. They know their jobs." Unlike Pa, who was more of a dreamer than a doer. The one dream he had that worked out was when he decided to start a draft mule business with a mammoth jack he'd won in a card game. He talked the local farmers who had quality draft horse mares into giving him one foal for every two breedings. The result was more than a dozen draft mule foals the next year, but then the war broke out.

Now his dream was to go to California. I had eight of the mules, the wagon, nowhere else to go, and I was happy to make up for lost time with my pa. He had the gift of gab and a hefty dollop of charm, which got me more than one well paying freight job. We had a light load this time, though –supplies for the trip west. But we had to take a detour to Wolf Creek to pick up a wagon he'd won playing euchre last week.

"You should let me drive for a while. The mules need to get used to me, now that we'll have two wagons and two teams."

"They'll figure it out once the time comes." Which I didn't think would come. Most of Pa's schemes didn't pan out. Besides, he didn't hold the reins right, even though I'd showed him ten times over.

"Think that widow woman would go with us?"

"Nope." The wagon that Pa won was at the loser's sister-in-law's place in Wolf Creek. He'd been speculating about her the whole way. All he knew was her husband got killed in the war.

"Pa, not everyone wants to go west. What would she do out there?"

"I hear there's ten men for every woman. She could find herself a rich husband. You could, too."

I gritted my teeth and kept my gaze aimed straight ahead. The war hadn't been easy on our family and truth was, I had no idea how to be a wife. The mules seemed a lot safer and a whole lot less stubborn than most men I'd ever met. They worked harder, too.

"Could. Won't hold my breath."

"I wish your ma and your brother was with us."

"Me, too." I missed them both something awful, but tried not to think about it much.

"Your ma wouldn't approve of you wearing man's clothes, though."

"She would if it kept us alive."

The war had been brutal to the Ozarks farmers. Our family and the neighbors had watched all our worldly possessions burn or be stolen. Many lost their lives –not from battles, but from bushwhackers and jayhawkers. Both sides. Most of the raiders were a bunch of outlaws looking for justification to do their dirty deeds.

A year before the war ended, my brother Zeb had disappeared from the field he was plowing. He'd only been fourteen years old, and the family never knew what happened to him. The neighbor boy, sixteen –same age as me –came up missing the same day.

A few months later, Ma had died when she ran back into our burning cabin to salvage the family's bed linens after some raiders had torched every building on our farm. Pa nearly died of the smoke when he tried to rescue her.

But just now, we had troubles of a different kind. A bullet whistled by my ear and then I heard the sharp crack of a rifle.

"A hold-up!" I yelled.

Four men, one riding on each side of the wagon and two gaining from behind, gave chase.

"Run, run, run!" The mules obeyed me, breaking into a full gallop, and I could only hope the four loose mules trailing behind stayed close.

"Pa, take over." I shoved the reins into Pa's hands and grabbed the double-barrel scattergun from the holster on the side of the seat. With a firm grip, I fired a shot at the man on the left, then squeezed off another round. The last one blew off his hat and slowed him down some. "Hand me the Henry."

The mules galloped as fast as they could pull, with the wagon flying over ruts and bumps. "It's blasted hard to shoot and stay set."

"You can't hit nothing with the wagon bouncing around like this." He passed the rifle to me anyway.

"Maybe not, but they'll have something to think about." I braced myself to cock it and aimed as best I could, firing the first round. The man on the right flinched –a graze that barely tore his shirt and not enough to do any good. He and the outlaws behind them closed in.

"Shoot his horse!" Pa said. "Bigger target."

"It ain't the horses I'm worried about." I fired another round at the man on the right. The scoundrels behind them moved up fast, pistols blazing.

"Stay low, Pa!"

The thief on the right fired three shots and Pa slouched to the side, nearly falling off. His eyes bugged out and beads of sweat dotted his forehead. Blood bubbled out of his chest.

"Pa!" I dropped the Henry, grabbed the back of his shirt, and dragged him back up, but he'd let go of the reins and they were trailing in the dirt. "Pa, are you alive?"

He didn't say a word. My arm strained as I hung onto him and my heart ached for my pa, my one last link to family, and the dearest part of my life. I just hoped more bullets didn't find us as the mules raced on and the wagon jerked and jolted. I hung onto Pa for all I was worth.

The other four mules weren't in sight. With a little luck and maybe a hand from the Big Man, I hoped they were all right, but mostly that my father was alive.

The two men rode alongside the team, grabbed the jerk line, and pulled them to a stop. The scruffy robber holding back the mules was older, mid-thirties maybe, but the younger, blond fellow appeared to be in charge. He had the weathered look of a man who spent more nights under the stars than not, and didn't seem to care that we saw his sneering face. If I lived through this, he'd regret that mistake.

"Throw down your guns and your money!"

I tossed my shotgun to the ground. "Ain't got any money."

"Get down and be real careful about it. The old man, too."

"He's shot. Hurt bad." Much as it tore me up to leave my father, I knew it wouldn't do a bit of good for me

157

to get shot, too, so I tried to make him as comfortable as I could and then climbed down.

The blond fellow bit off a hunk of chaw and leaned his forearm on the saddlehorn. "What's in the wagon?"

Everything we owned, which wasn't much. "Flour, salt –supplies for the kitchen."

The old one rode to the wagon, reached down, and flipped up the canvas. "Yep, nothing worth a nickel."

The leader spat. "Eh, I'll take your mules, then. Looks like I could get a good price."

"You can't do that! I've gotta take my pa to the doctor. He's hurt bad."

The old man stared at Pa for a bit and shrugged. "If he ain't dead already, he will be shortly."

"He needs a doctor."

The blond one waved his revolver at me. "Step back from the wagon." He nodded at his partner. "Cut the leather and make sure it ain't usable. I'll tie the mules to a lead line." Then, training his revolver on Pa, he said, "Girlie, you move a muscle and I'll put a bullet through the old fart's gullet."

He drew his other pistol with his left hand and fired three shots in the air. While the older outlaw sliced the harness leather, the other two outlaws rode in, kicking up dirt and dust.

"Bring in those four loose mules," the leader told them. "I know where we can sell them."

"Yes, sir!" They pivoted their horses and took off at a full gallop.

When the older fellow finished cutting the harness off the team, they balked.

"C'mon!" He yanked on the rope he'd tied around Zeus's neck. Poseidon took umbrage and kicked the man in the shins. The foul-mouthed robber hopped around and cussed a blue streak as the blond fellow lashed both mules with his quirt.

Any man who'd treat an animal like that was lower than gopher poop. While I couldn't tolerate a man who was mean to animals, the mules needed to cooperate so none of them got hurt. "Zeus, Poseidon, calm down. Hermes and Hephaestus, you follow along, now."

The mules looked at me and snorted their disagreement.

"You be good boys. I'll be along shortly."

With a scowl, the older man mounted his horse. He waved his rope at the mules. "H'yaw."

As I watched those two dirty rotten thieves take away four of my best friends in the world, it all hit me –Pa was next thing to dead, I had no plans of my own, and the dollar and fourteen cents in my vest pocket wasn't enough to pay a doctor, rent a hotel room, and buy feed for the mules. Or me.

I scrambled back on the wagon to tend to Pa. He didn't even moan from pain, which worried me even more, and blood soaked his clothes and the seat. At least they didn't take my Henry. It was on the floorboard of the wagon where I'd dropped it when Pa was hit. Since those other two would be riding up any minute, I grabbed some cartridges and reloaded.

Pa bled something terrible so I grabbed my spare shirt and used it for bandages. Nothing would stop the bleeding, though, and life was leaving him, sure as shootin'. I didn't have time to mourn, but I did get mad. I jumped off the wagon and flung my hat on the ground, swearing those miserable turds would answer to justice. I wanted to see them hang.

I heard hooves pounding and felt the earth shake. My mules were coming at me at a dead run. Such big animals running straight at you can be a dang sight scary, but I knew they'd protect me. Mules ain't like horses, who shy and run from everything. A mule will stand and fight if he thinks he has a chance.

They formed a circle around me to protect me from the two low-down crooks bent on taking everything important to me, including my father's life. He was still on the wagon seat –couldn't do any more for him except get him to a doctor, if he could make it that far.

I stepped between the front mules, Aries and Apollo, and made sure the two men saw the business end of my rifle.

"Hold it right there, you good-for-nothing rascals. Throw your weapons down. All of them –pistols, knives, rifles –anything you got." I trained the rifle on the bigger one. "Get off your horses, and keep your hands where I can see them. Try me, and this one dies."

I ain't too keen on killing a man, but if it was them or me, then they'd be buzzard pickings. They weren't dismounting. That made me even madder.

"This here Henry's quite a rifle –I can fire off a dozen shots with it in less than a minute."

I guess that done it because they hit the ground quick, hands out. Once they dismounted, I got a clearer look at the pair. The big one stood over six feet tall judging by his horse, which I reckoned to be sixteen hands or better –he was almost as big as my smallest mule. The outlaw had a handsome face and broad shoulders –more than likely thought he was God's gift to women, but he also seemed familiar. He stood spraddle-legged like a man who'd spent more time in the saddle than on the ground.

The shorter one gawked at me and I stared back at him. There was no mistaking that face and those blue eyes –a younger version of Obadiah Parry. Brown hair parted like Pa's, and standing the same with his weight on his left leg as Pa did when he was younger. He was a couple inches taller, though. Close to six feet, likely.

He blinked as if he was waking up from a nightmare. "Don't I know you?"

"Zeb?" I couldn't decide whether to hug him or shoot him.

"Elsie?"

For a moment we sized each other up. "My own brother is stealing my mules and robbing us?"

"Dang, Elsie, put that gun down! I'll explain."

He had a whole lot of explaining to do. "Who's your friend?"

"You know him, too. Hank Lockhart."

Hank was the neighbor boy who'd disappeared the same day as my brother. "What in tarnation are you doing in Kansas, scaring folks half to death and taking what ain't yours?"

"I'll tell you if you put that gun down."

"You'll tell me anyhow. We gotta get Pa to the doctor –your other friend like as killed him already. Blood's pouring out of his chest. He might've expired while we're standing here talking."

Zeb raised his hands. "Don't shoot, Sis. But I want to see my pa."

I waved him over to Pa with the rifle barrel. "You, too, Hank. I want you both in the same spot. Easier to shoot you that way. And you know sure as coyotes howl that I can hit what I'm aiming at."

"Yes, I remember." Hank followed Zeb to the wagon, and the mules followed Hank. One suspicious move and they'd be all over him, and I reckoned he knew enough about mules to understand that.

My brother petted Obadiah on the forehead. "Pa?"

The old man gurgled and winced, then his lips curled into a gruesome smile. "My boy... came home." And then he breathed his last.

I got all choked up and danged near started to cry but I didn't want tears interfering with my aiming, so I blinked them back as best I could. Our pa wasn't the best pa in the world, but he was our only pa. He loved us and we loved him —there was never a doubt.

When I got to where I could talk, I said, "Ain't a day gone by but what Pa didn't find some reason to mention you, Zeb. He never forgot about you and never gave up hope. I'm glad he didn't know what come of you."

"I ain't a bit proud of it." Zeb hung his head. "Back on the farm, spring of '64, me'n Hank was plowing, when some soldiers came down on us, rifles pointed right at us. Asked what side we was on and Hank said, 'Your side.' They didn't wear uniforms, just regular clothes, so we didn't know. Pa never took sides and I paid no mind. Just didn't want to get shot. Turns out, we hooked up with

162

some bushwhackers and some of them, including us, went with the Danby gang after the war."

I nodded, hoping he didn't think I was judging, for we're not to do that, but it was hard to believe my own brother was one of the raiders that burned our family out of house and home. Even if he wasn't with the scoundrels who burned our place, how many families had he ruined? Still, I could see that a fourteen-year-old boy wouldn't have much choice in the matter, whether bushwhackers or jayhawkers, if they decided he was to ride with them.

"You've explained one year. How about the six years since?"

Hank shrugged. "We didn't have nothing to do nor money or way to get any, and with what we done during the war, we didn't want to go back home."

"I can't believe the boy who rescued orphan bunnies would turn to hurting people."

He studied the dirt, but didn't utter a word. I sensed there must be some good left in him deep down.

"You were sixteen when they took you, Hank. That'd put you at twenty-three now. Are you ready to be a man yet?"

"Are you gonna put that Henry down?" Zeb asked.

"Don't know's I can trust either of you. Yayhoos like you ruined our family and our neighbors, too."

Zeb's cheek flinched, just like it had when our mama used to holler at him for chasing the chickens. "We ain't gonna hurt you, Sis."

"Well, you two should be ashamed of yourselves. And it's stopping right here, right now, you hear?"

"Yes, ma'am," both men muttered.

"Right this minute." I lowered the rifle, but still had it at the ready. "We got things to do. First, Pa needs burying –we'll take him to the undertaker at Wolf Creek. Second, we're getting those mules back from your two friends who thought they needed them more than me. Third, we're turning your friends over to the law."

Zeb pushed his hat up and his cheek flinched. "They're probably already hooked up with some of the others."

"We'll do what we have to do. And fourth, we're going to California. Pa wanted to see the Pacific Ocean before he breathed his last. Well, he didn't, but that don't mean we can't take a lock of his hair there. Besides, you two need to get out of here, away from these hard cases you call friends. They'll think you turned color on them, anyway, so's best you make yourselves scarce."

Hank's horse nudged him on the back and he patted the side of the animal's head. "Where's your pa's bedroll? We can wrap him up in it and tie him onto the saddle. I'll walk."

"Good idea." I fetched Pa's blankets from the wagon and gave them to Hank.

"Hank and me will take care of Pa," Zeb said. "We'll put him on my horse, though. I'll walk."

"Ain't none of us walking." My brother did the right thing by offering, but I had four mules so we might as well use them. "There's a saddle in the wagon. We'll put Pa on Plato –he's the calmest of the herd. I'll ride Apollo."

"You named your mules after the Greek gods in Ma's book."

"Yep. A little something to remember her by every day."

"I'm sorely grieved at her passing." His shoulders sagged. "At first I thought you was her. You're a spittin' image –your hair and all."

"That's a high compliment." I left it at that, but Ma was a beautiful woman and muleskinners ain't. Granted, my hair favored hers –dark brown and near to my waist when I let it down.

Ma had gone to Heaven nearly seven years ago, so I had plenty of time to get used to the idea of her passing, but for Zeb, it was a new wound on top of just losing our pa. I patted his shoulder. "Ma always held hope you'd come back to us, so she'd be happy we're together today." Although she wouldn't have been a bit happy about how we got together.

Hank brushed down the two sweaty horses and resaddled them. "Got any water?"

"Not for the animals –just a little in a canteen, but we ain't far from Wolf Creek. There's a good livery there."

He helped Zeb wrap Pa while I saddled Plato. Hefting a saddle on an eighteen-hand mule can be a trial, but I got it done. When the men finished with Pa, I told the mule to hold still. "You have to be extra special careful, now. This is Pa you're hauling."

Plato had to think about things. Another person might say he's balky, but he ain't. Once he figured out what you wanted him to do, he'd do it –long as it wasn't something stupid –and he'd probably get it done better than the way you thought he ought to go about it.

165

"Are you riding a mule?" Zeb asked. "You can ride my horse and I'll walk."

"I'm riding Apollo. He's the one with the front stockings." Apollo tossed his head and whinny-brayed, making sure they knew exactly who he was.

Once we had Pa tied on, Zeb and Hank started to mount.

"You could help a lady up. Apollo's a mighty tall animal."

Hank came over to give me a boost, but once he had me in mid-air, he asked, "Where's your saddle?"

"Under Pa. That's the only one we –er, I have. But don't pay that no mind. I've rode all these mules bareback."

I had to argue with Zeb and Hank both, Hank holding me about a foot off the ground. They thought I should ride a horse and they'd ride bareback, but I finally convinced them that Apollo and Plato would do as I asked. Whether they'd pay mind to strangers, I didn't know, but likely not.

Once we all got mounted, I told Apollo to find his brothers. Truth be told, the men were harder to convince than the mules. Talk about stubborn.

We left the wagon since the harnesses were worthless, and everything I owned except the mules was in it. I hoped no one stole it, but neither could I afford to leave a man behind. Once we came upon the two dirty devils who murdered my pa and stole my mules, I'd need both men and then some.

I rode out, Hank beside me, Zeb behind him, and Plato behind me.

"They'd be at the farmhouse by now," Hank said. "Our orders are to meet up with them there, just east of Wolf Creek." Hank and Zeb traded glances. They weren't telling me something important, and my guess was that the bunch of them planned to rob the citizens of Wolf Creek.

"Them mules don't like to be away from me, and I expect they're dawdling."

We rode for quarter of an hour or so when we sighted the farmhouse up ahead. The horses and mules needed water but we weren't sure of what sort of hospitality we'd find there.

As we neared, Zeb told us to stop and dismount. Hermes tried to make a snack of my hair and I batted him off.

"Why not ride in?"

"Because it's time for evening chores and there's not one person moving. Animals are fussing to get fed and the cows are bawling to be milked." He cocked his head to the side. "Best we take the animals behind that knoll so's they ain't seen."

Apollo's ears pricked up. He lifted his head and bared his teeth, sniffing the air. The other three mules did the same.

"I think the mules smell their brothers." The mules and I followed Zeb and Hank to the hiding spot he'd pointed to. When we got there, I said, "That cinches it. We've found our men. Now to take them to the marshal."

"It ain't that easy, Elsie. We don't know where they are –in the house or the barn –and we don't know if they're holding the farmer and maybe his family if he has one –Hank and I haven't been to the house before. We

167

rode by so we know it's the right one, but we don't know if the family who lives there is partial to Danby, or is being held by Maggert and Dickey. Or..."

His voice trailed off. I knew what the "or" meant. Dead bodies.

Zeb squinted. "Don't see any horses so they must be in the barn. I'd say the farmer has a wife because there's a flower garden to the side of the house. Don't see no toys, but there still could be young'uns."

His tone made me think that it was their normal way of doing things –taking whatever they wanted from anyone handy, and not worrying much about the dead they left behind.

"There's two outlaws and three of us."

Hank stepped beside me, holding his horse's reins. "There's three of us all right, but only two fighters, and there could be five of them. We was to meet up with the others here. Danby planned to shut down the town and rob the bank. We're the second wave through."

I hated to think of what he meant by shutting down the town. As for fighting, I wasn't too keen on the idea, but if it came to that, I'd be in the fray.

"So first thing we need is to know how many and where they are."

"Yep," agreed Zeb. "And that's my job. Been doing it for seven years. Learned from an Indian tracker."

"All right, but we ain't killing anybody, so get that through your head. We're taking them in. They'll swing legal-like."

They didn't go along with that, I could tell by Hank's smirk and the way Zeb clenched his jaw.

"You two have done enough killing and rabble rousing."

My brother adjusted his gun belt and loaded his revolver. Watching him brought home to me that he wasn't a fun boy anymore, but a man used to handling weapons and not averse to using them. It made me sad. He fetched some things out of his saddlebags but I couldn't see what. "I'll be taking a look now," he said. "Hank, keep her quiet."

That last remark made my hairline sizzle but I let it slide. He skulked around the knoll, using the prairie grass for cover, and I could tell he was skilled. He didn't know that I'd spent a year on the mountain, just me and the mules, and I had to fend for myself.

A body's hungry belly is a powerful teacher when it comes to trapping. You have to be quiet and patient. Neither comes natural to me but I learned them, along with how to skin anything from a porcupine to a deer –whatever I caught.

Pa'd given me the Henry but told me not to use it for fear the rifle report would bring unwanted guests –and anyone except him was unwanted. That meant I had to catch my supper in a quiet way. It also meant I became downright handy with the bowie knife.

"Hank," I whispered. "I got an idea. We ain't got a chance in a gunfight, and you two need to stop killing, anyway, so we're gonna trap those yayhoos –real quiet-like."

He tilted his chin down and studied me. Those brown eyes of his could lull a body into thinking he's agreeable, but I could see he had his own plans, which likely meant a couple more dead folks to haul to the undertaker.

He hunkered down on his belly and crawled to the knoll crest. I told the mules to stay put and crawled up there with him.

"You see any of your friends yet?"

"They ain't my friends. Zeb is, but the rest are all mean as three-legged badgers."

"Tell me about them."

"The leader is Maggert. You met him already. The fellow with him, his lapdog, is Dickey. There could be three more –can't tell because I can't see the inside of the barn so I don't know which horses are there."

"It's awful quiet." That made me even more uneasy. "Who are the other three and why weren't they with you?"

"Bird, Yancy, and Cross. They had business in Wichita and said they'd meet up with us east of Wolf Creek. Could be here. Bird's good with a blade, Yancy's a sharpshooter, and Cross is Yancy's man."

I hated to ask the next question, but I needed to know. "If they're all there, what do you suppose is going on?"

"Hard to say. Might be cooking supper. Could've killed the man of the house, maybe any young'uns, and saving the woman for later."

My heart went out to the family even though we didn't even know for sure there was one. I well knew the fear of seeing your kin killed and your farm burned.

"I guess we'll find out when Zeb gets back."

Hank pointed, and I saw Zeb crouched behind the

barn. Even though my brother had been riding with a bunch of bad apples, I hoped he'd take care. I just got him back and didn't want to lose him again.

The mules were restless and I had to shush them a time or two. You can't fool a mule –they always know when something's amiss. The sun beat down on us and our patience wore thin fast, but we'd have enough action to suit us all real soon.

Finally, Zeb came back. I handed him the canteen and waited for him to take a long pull. He wiped his mouth on his sleeve and squatted. With a stick, he drew a map of the farmstead.

"Bird, Yancy, and Cross are here. Their horses are still wet so they can't have been here for but half an hour or less. Right now they're in the house with Maggert and Dickey, reporting on the bank in Wichita." He jabbed the corner of the sketch of the house. "That's our next job if Danby doesn't take us to Indian Territory after the Wolf Creek job."

"Which he will." Hank had a wrinkle in his brow that told me he didn't like something Zeb had either said or not said. "Did you hear them talking?"

Zeb nodded. "They're waiting for us, but plan to leave as soon as the horses are rested, with us or without. They don't seem to pay no mind about us."

"Which ain't true." Hank smirked. "We know the only ones who leave the Danby gang are dead."

That news didn't exactly perk up my day. "Which is the one who killed Pa?"

"It'd be either Maggert or Dickey."

"The older one."

"That's Dickey, but mind you he don't do a thing unless Maggert tells him to, so Maggert pulled the trigger just as sure as the other'n."

Same as he told Dickey to cut the harnesses. A man like that had no feelings for right or wrong. "Then we'll bring them both to justice."

"Maybe." Hank drew a square in the dirt. "Or we'll have to kill all five before they kill all three of us." He handed the stick to Zeb. "Show me the layout of the barn and what's where."

"There's more ways to solve a problem than killing people," I reminded Zeb and Hank. "We're bringing them to the law." Zeb petted me on the head as if I was ignorant of the ways of the world. Maybe I was, but their time for killing was over.

Hank went on like I hadn't said a word. "You take the back window and I'll draw them out front."

"There's more," Zeb said, drawing a circle around the corner of the sketched farmhouse. "The farmer's there on the floor –don't know if he's dead or not. His wife is cooking. Didn't see any young'uns but that don't mean there ain't any."

I had to speak up. "That woman deserves better, and killing will only make it worse for her. No, we're gonna trap those varmints. I have an idea." I laid out my notion of how things ought to go. It took some convincing but I'm used to working with mules and eventually they agreed.

"Pa will have to wait for us here." I told Zeb to lift the body down, and then I took the saddle off Plato.

"I don't think he's going anywhere," Zeb said.

172

"Just the same, we won't take long if this hare-brain scheme works out."

The farmstead lay on the south side of the road, with the house closest to the knoll where we were. It was about fifty yards from a good-size barn, twice as big as the house. The yard in between was hard-packed dirt with a well in the middle, and the privy was behind the house. I saw a wagon to the north side of the barn, and two big corrals on the south side –one with my mules in it and the other with a pony and four Jersey cows. Not a single tree grew anywhere. How these people lived without trees was beyond me.

All three of us stayed in the prairie grass, circled around the farmstead, and entered the barn from the back. The mules in the corral whinny-brayed and I knew they'd seen me so I motioned for them to stay.

Hank opened the back barn door taking care not to make any noise. I plastered myself against the wall right beside the door while Zeb opened the stall gates and led the horses out –four on one side and one on the other.

Zeb sneaked up to the house window as if he was half mountain lion and motioned for Hank, who ran and crouched behind the wagon. I climbed up the ladder to the hayloft, armed with a rope, my Henry, and my bowie knife.

When Zeb waved, I hooted. The mules had played hide-and-seek with me when we were stuck on the mountain. I'd hide and hoot, then the mules would come looking for me. We hadn't played the game in a while, but I counted on them remembering. When they didn't come, I admit to getting a might worried, so I hooted again, a little louder. Then I heard the welcome thumping of hooves and I knew the mules were jumping the fence.

Hephaestus and Hermes came first. I held my hand up motioning for them to stay still, which they did. When Zeus and Poseidon trotted up, I said, "Chase!" They jumped around like little puppies, then charged the horses, nipping them on the backside until they ran out the front. Hank shooed them to the side of the house and the mules took over.

"Run!" I yelled. The horses and mules pounded the ground –I could even feel it in the hayloft. Four men came out of the house and Zeb went in. I wished him luck –he'd be taking down Maggert, he reckoned, and it looked like he was right. I hoped the woman had enough sense to stay out of the way.

Hank had run behind the well, and when the four men ran out, he tripped Dickey, and while the scoundrel was eating dirt, Hank disarmed him. I threw the rope down and he hogtied Dickey in record time.

I let out a whistle and the other four mules came at a gallop. "Kick!" I yelled, pointing out to the field where the other animals were. The three men lagged behind, probably realizing they needed to go back for ropes. With luck, they wouldn't get that chance.

What worried me was whether those men would start shooting at my mules. Somehow, I needed to get the horses between them, figuring they wouldn't shoot their own mounts.

Hank ran into the house where I heard all manner of crashing and carrying on. I ran to the tied-up man and checked to make sure he couldn't get away.

174

"Ain't such a tough man now, are you?" I said. I wanted to spit on him in the worst way but didn't. He'd get what was coming to him from the law.

He chuckled –the low, evil kind. "Is the old man dead yet?"

"You know the answer, and you know you're gonna hang." I left him there in the dirt. If the horses and mules came back by, he might get stepped on a little. Would be a shame.

A bullet whistled by and lodged in the barn wood. I hit the ground and belly-crawled to the barn as fast as I could, then climbed the ladder to the hayloft and knelt beside the mow door. Zeb had made me promise not to get myself in a situation where I put them and the woman in even more risk. I got that.

Dickey hollered and one of the outlaws ran toward him. The mules chased the others, biting and kicking. I wouldn't want to be those men. Problem is, those blamed mules were sending them my way. But I couldn't let that other man free Dickey. I cocked the Henry and aimed for his foot.

Just as I was about to squeeze the trigger, someone grabbed the back of my shirt. I scooped up my bowie knife and held it tight to my leg. He turned me around and held my arms to my sides. I'd dropped the Henry but still had the knife.

"Looking for trouble, girlie?" It was Maggert. Zeb and Hank was supposed to have took care of him. I figured that Zeb couldn't hold him and Hank didn't get there in time.

I heard stomping and whinnying, and braying in

the yard but couldn't tell what happened. Gunfire and cursing. But I was looking into the face of my pa's murderer.

"I'm taking you to justice, Maggert."

"You and that turncoat brother of yours?"

"How'd you know that?"

"You both look like your pa. That's why I left him and Lockhart out there with you. Reckoned you'd talk him into gunning for me."

"Smart feller." The longer I kept him talking, the more time I had to think. "What if that weren't so?"

"If not, they'd follow orders."

I saw a frying pan over his head and heard a clunk when it hit. Maggert turned around to see what the annoyance was, and I poked the bowie knife tip into his back. A tall, thin dark-haired woman stood there ready to swing the skillet again.

"You pick, Maggert," I said. "A knife in your back or another walloping with the skillet."

He chuckled. "I bet you're as squeamish as your brother. Can't finish off anyone, including me. If he wasn't such a good tracker, I'd have got rid of him long ago."

I pushed the knife in a little farther, and blood soaked his shirt. "The female of the species is always more vicious. Wanna give me a try?"

I wanted him to give me a reason to push that knife in even more. It came to me that that's what the "judge not" was all about. It wasn't up to me to decide if Zeb and Hank had done wrong. This man was a killer, but the law would decide his fate, not me. Even so, I wanted him to

176

give me a reason to whittle a little piece out of his back.

"Take his pistol," I told the woman.

She looked a like a rabbit sneaking up on a wolf, kind of stepping sideways and reaching out. Maggert grabbed her hand. She gasped. I poked. He roared. She clonked him over the head with that frying pan again and again. Finally he fell.

"Go get some rope, or leather straps –whatever you can find."

She scampered off, and looked ever so happy to get away. I still held the knife to Maggert's neck, thinking he'd wake up soon. She hadn't hit him that hard, and the knife wound wasn't deep.

The woman climbed up the ladder with a rope and a pony saddle. "Thought we could tie his hands, then cinch him up in this to keep his arms tight."

"Good thinking. My name's Elsie. You?"

"Mary."

Maggert was already coming around by the time we got his hands bound. Mary threw that saddle over his chest, I flipped the man over, and we cinched him up good and proper. I had a goodly long tail left on the rope so I wound it around his legs and boots.

"Mary, get your frying pan and stand right here. He moves a muscle, you bash him on the head again. Keep it up until you pound some reason into him." I checked his pistol to see if it was loaded. It was, and I handed it to her. "If you think he might get loose, shoot him in the legs."

I worried about my brother and Hank. After I wiped off my knife and picked up the Henry, I climbed down the ladder. The stomping and hollering had quieted so I had no way of knowing who was where.

Dickey still lay in the dirt –tied, tattered, and groaning. I stepped over him and headed to the house. Two scoundrels bagged, three to go.

Not a sound came from the house. The door was ajar and I peeked in. Two men lay on the floor –one was likely Mary's husband. Someone grabbed me and jammed his hand over my mouth.

"Elsie, it's me, Hank. I'm letting you go."

I breathed easier. "You with them? Or us?"

"You know the answer to that. Bird's dead." He nodded toward a body on the floor. "Yancy and Cross have Zeb. They took off across the field out back."

"Horses?"

"They haven't caught them yet that I know of."

"Best we see if they found yours and Zeb's horses behind the knoll. I'll call the mules."

By then, we heard hoofbeats –lots of them. I put my pinky fingers between my teeth and whistled and the next moment, we were surrounded by eight draft mules. On top of Poseidon was a bloodied Zeb, hanging on to the scraggly mane for dear life.

Hank hauled him down and set him on the porch. "Where's Yancy and Cross?"

"Cross is out in the field, trompled." He wiped blood off his forehead with his sleeve. "Don't know about Yancy or Rhodes."

"Rhodes?"

"Didn't see him. Must be getting sloppy. When I went into the house, both Maggert and Rhodes laid into me. I didn't think Hank would ever get there. Before he did, Rhodes hauled me out back. They planned to shoot me, but the mules came running through and the one stopped long enough for me to get on. I don't know how I got on that big beast, but if you're scared enough, you can do blamed near anything."

"Let's collect Cross, then," I said, happy to see my brother alive. I wanted to know more but we had business to take care of. "The farmer's wife, Mary, has Maggert up in the hayloft. Lucky for me, she wasn't shy about using her frying pan. Dickey's in the yard where we left him. I say we leave Yancy and Rhodes –take the three we have to the law in Wolf Creek, and haul Cross and Bird to the undertaker. We have to go there anyhow for Pa."

The mules trotted to the corral and jumped in.

"What in tarnation are those animals doing?" Zeb asked.

"Drinking. The trough's in the corral." I sure wished we had the wagon –then I remembered the farm wagon north of the barn. "I'll ask Mary if they have a harness big enough for draft mules. We can haul them all in the wagon."

"I'll go check on the farmer," Hank said. "He was still alive last I knew. We can take him to the doctor there."

I leaned the Henry against the house, sat beside my brother, and brushed some weeds and dirt out of his hair. To Hank, I said, "Best go spell Mary and have her tend to her husband. But be careful, she swings one mean frying pan. Maggert's tied up. Once we get the wagon in front of the barn, you can roll him out and let him fall."

"You said you didn't want any killing."

179

"I didn't say nothing about maiming. We'll put straw in the wagon."

Hank and I found the tack, harnessed two of the mules, and fixed up the wagon bed with straw and blankets. He lowered Maggert with a rope, so he didn't have a bumpy ride after all. You'd never know it by all his hollering, though. Zeb helped load Dickey and Bird's body, then they left to pick up Pa's body, and after that, they'd circle around to the field and pick up Cross.

I pumped some water and helped Mary as she fussed over her husband, Virgil. He'd fared better than it had looked, and was able to stand. Shaky, but upright.

"Reckoned if they thought I was alive, it'd be harder on Mary." He was likely right about that, and he looked almost human once she washed his face.

His wife nodded toward the window. "The wagon's in the field now."

Good, because I was worried about the two that got away. "We didn't catch Yancy and Rhodes." They might've caught their horses and joined up with the Danby gang in Wolf Creek. My hope was they wouldn't go after Zeb and Hank. The sooner we were quit of this country, the better. The Pacific Ocean was sounding mighty fine.

"Your men better take care. Yancy bragged about his long-distance shooting." Virgil, still not too steady on his feet, carefully lowered himself onto a kitchen chair and admired my Henry. "Sure wished I'd had one of those during the war. Might have saved some of my friends."

Mary pulled back the curtain pointed out the window to the top of the knoll. "I think your men are in trouble."

180

Sure enough, a rifle barrel poked through the grass. I could see Hank and Zeb out in the field tying up Cross. Sitting ducks. I grabbed the rifle. Mary and Virgil were about to see a little distance shooting, too.

Mary took the window glass out. "Looks like Yancy's waiting for the fellows to move to the other side of the wagon so he has a clean shot."

I prayed Zeb and Hank stayed right where they were until I could get set. I planted my elbows on the window sill, tucked the stock tight to my shoulder, and concentrated on quieting my heart. My breathing was shallow but even. I calmed my eyeballs and took careful aim just behind Yancy's barrel. Then, on an out breath, squeezed the trigger.

Pans rattled and the boom nearly deafened us all. I hit the target dead on –the rifle barrel flew in the air, splintered, and a few rounds went off besides. Hank and Zeb crouched behind the wagon, pistols drawn, thinking someone from the house shot at them.

I cocked and set to fire again if need be. The grass rustled on the knoll, two shots were fired –pistol, not rifle. Hank and Zeb turned toward the sound. At least they were pointed the right direction. I didn't have a clear shot but as it was, Hank and Zeb had nothing but a wagon and two mules between them and death.

That did it. Those yayhoos had killed my Ma, my Pa, and turned my baby brother into a murderer. They weren't getting anything more. When the grass rustled again, I aimed and fired, cocked, and fired again. Nine cartridges left. Now it was their turn.

Maggert managed to wiggle out of the wagon and

181

ran for his buddies, still trussed up in the pony saddle. One of them ran down the knoll, firing as he went. Looked like he didn't hit anything but dirt, but I couldn't be sure, and I didn't have a clear shot at either of them.

I whistled for the mules, and they took off, wagon and all, back for the house.

Hank and Zeb split up and went at the two scoundrels from either side. Zeb tackled Rhodes but not before Rhodes had managed to uncinch Maggert. We should've done a better job. He still had his hands tied but he used them for a club on my brother. Zeb went down and bounced right back up, taking Maggert's legs as he stood, but getting a hefty kick in the gut.

Hank and the other one fought fast and brutal. They hit each other so hard, I could hear bones cracking even though they were a couple hundred yards away.

At the sound of a muffled shot, Zeb went down and stayed. I tried to stay calm so my shooting would be on target, but if he killed my brother I'd see justice done sooner rather than later.

I aimed but couldn't get off a shot before Maggert jumped Hank, clubbing him from behind with his bound hands. Hank twirled around and kicked Maggert in the ribs and he went down. If Hank would just take off and run, I could hit Maggert, but he fought on.

The mules pulled the wagon into the yard. "Mary, take your frying pan and make sure Dickey behaves himself."

To get Hank's attention, I aimed about a foot from Maggert's head and fired. But at that moment, Maggert jumped up and took a bullet in the thigh. I felt real bad for that scalawag.

It was enough to distract the other bushwhacker. Hank knocked him down and twisted his arm behind his back. Just to make the dirty devil behave, I fired off another round, kicking up dirt about three feet from him. Hank threw the man's pistol and a knife away from them.

My stomach churned knowing my brother could be dead or dying out there. I ran outside and jumped on the wagon.

"Mary, do you have any rope in the house?"

She nodded and ran in to fetch it.

The reins were all messed up but I fished them out enough to get us going, and by then Mary had thrown the rope in the back. I hollered at the mules to get on with it. A minute later, we stopped by my brother, who was sitting in the dirt holding his bloody arm. I hated to see him hurt but I was so blamed glad he was alive that tears welled in my eyes.

I nodded at him and took the rope over to Hank, figuring we needed to get the last one trussed up before tending to Zeb. "Is this Yancy?"

"Nope, Rhodes."

"Yancy's dead," Rhodes said, more of a groan since Hank's knee was firmly planted in his back. "Sharpshooter got him."

Hank raised an eyebrow and gazed at me. "It's fitting he should go out that way." He cocked his head toward Zeb. "Best tend to your brother. He's leaking."

Maggert was bleeding, too, but I didn't much care. His hands were still tied.

"Might as well saddle him up again," I told Hank.

183

"We don't have any more rope.

Hank's face looked like a meat pie but he fared a whole lot better than Rhodes, who had a couple of missing teeth and a crooked, bloody nose. His left eye was swollen shut, and he babied his broken left arm with his right.

We'd had a long afternoon. Hank and I put Rhodes and Cross in the wagon. Cross had expired and Rhodes didn't want to ride with dead bodies, but Hank explained to him that they didn't talk much. I told the mules to get back in the corral and wait for us.

Half an hour later, we pulled into Wolf Creek. The smell of burning animals and the sight of blood churned my belly. The place looked like hell on earth with dead mules, horses, and people scattered all over. We couldn't even get into town without clearing the road. Hank and I unhitched the wagon and used the mules to pull the dead animals to the side of the street. Zeb couldn't help much on account of the bullet in his arm.

Once we finally did get in town, I asked for the doctor.

"He rode with the posse," said a bloody, dazed man standing on the street, "but there's a dentist here who might tend your wounded. You'll have to get in line."

I told Hank we'd drop Zeb off at the dentist, then take the others to the jail, which we did. Zeb would have a long wait, but so it went. All this pain and misery was caused by the Danby gang, and if it weren't for them holding up my wagon, my brother and Hank would've been part of the horrible bloodbath.

The only lawman left in town was a deputy marshal, but I reckoned he could take care of business.

Hank wasn't too keen on visiting the law, with good reason, but we had to do the right thing.

Maggert had a good bit of swagger when he'd had his thumb on other men, but now he squawked like a scalded goose. "He's your man," he hollered, pointing at Hank. "Arrest him for stealing, murder, anything you can think of, he done it."

"Hank's not the one who murdered my father," I told Deputy Croy. "Maggert gave the order and Dickey pulled the trigger. But Hank's the one who brought my pa's murderers in."

The deputy had his hands full without listening to Maggert's whining, punctuated with nasty jabs by Dickey and Rhodes, both implicating Maggert all the way.

Croy shoved all three in a jail cell. "The dentist will be around eventually, after he sees to the honest folk." To Hank, he said, "Get on out of here. I'll take the lady's word on you, but only because I don't have time to look in on it."

He took the other bodies off our hands, too, so only Pa was left and we drove to the undertaker's. He gave me an envelope to hold a lock of Pa's hair. My dollar and fourteen cents didn't go far, and we still had to buy a harness, fetch my wagon, and visit the widow woman to pick up the wagon Pa had won. Whether it came with a harness, I didn't know. Harnesses seemed in short supply these days.

We picked up Zeb. His arm was bandaged and in a sling.

"I hope he's better at pulling teeth than he is at digging out bullets," he mumbled as he climbed on the

185

wagon. "But I got us a job."

"What?"

"Helping clean up. They need mules to right the wagons and get them where they belong, and all the dead animals have to be drug out to the pit some men are digging outside of town. First thing, we have to pick up a fresno at the blacksmith's shop and help dig."

"Zeb, I do believe you inherited Pa's gift of gab."

"That's a fact," Hank muttered. I expect he'd been the target of Zeb's blarney for the past seven years.

"We get a cut rate at the livery, and free meals."

"Even at a cut rate, we can't afford the livery. I spent my dollar and fourteen cents at the undertaker's."

"Don't you worry about that," my brother said. "I told them we wouldn't take any money, but if they have some harnesses laying around, we could sure use them. They told me to take a harness off the mules at the edge of town. Maybe we can find something to sell or trade for the livery fee."

Hank scowled. "Don't you think it best we skedaddle before they decide to lock us up?"

"Nope," I said. "Your time for running from the law is over."

We took the wagon back to Mary and Virgil, hooked the new harness up to our wagon, and came back to town, ready to work.

\*\*\*

Hank and I sweated buckets the next two days – both from the hard work and the hot sun. Zeb mostly supervised, what with his broken arm and his strong kinship to Pa's aversion to work, but he sweated, too, especially when he saw a badge. By the end of the job, they'd even stopped flinching every time they saw Deputy Croy.

The Imperial Hotel put us up and provided free baths, which we sorely needed. We ate fine meals at Ma's Café and met some nice folks. By the time the job was done, we'd made friends that I'd always remember.

If I hadn't promised Pa that I'd take him to the Pacific Ocean, Wolf Creek would be a place to consider settling. Not to be, though. I had a lock of Pa's hair and we were headed west.

The next morning, I hitched four mules to my wagon with Hank's help. It was nice not to do everything myself. The new harness was a lot better quality than my old one, thanks to the town citizens. Hank saddled his horse and Zeb's, too. I thought he might want to ride in the wagon what with his arm and all, but he insisted he could mount up himself.

After we get set to leave, I asked Hank, "Got any plans?"

"Farming in Oregon sounds good."

"Zeb?"

"Sounds good to me, too."

"Oregon's on the Pacific Ocean so I'm all right with that. Let's get the wagon from the widow woman and head out."

Zeb cleared his throat. "We have to pick up a load from the train first."

I could tell by the way his cheek flinched that he'd been up to his handiwork again. "What load?"

"The one we're taking to Kearney. It's right on the

187

way, and for good pay."

"We could use the cash."

"I suppose I have to do all the loading," Hank grumbled.

An hour later, we drove west out of Wolf Creek and then I pointed the mules north to hook up with the Oregon Trail. My brother, my friend, my mules, and me.

We looked forward to a more peaceful time.

THE END

## NEW BEGINNINGS
### By
### James J. Griffin

Ben Tolliver, his Stetson pulled low over his eyes, was dozing in a tilted-back chair in front of his livery stable. His pet paint, Cholla, was next to him, munching on hay. Ben had unbuttoned his shirt, allowing the afternoon sun to warm his chest and belly. Those warm rays sure felt good on his still-healing stomach wound.

Ben stirred when Cholla gave a soft warning nicker. He let the chair drop, shoved back his hat, and came to his feet as two men approached. One of the pair was Sheriff G.W. Satterlee.

"Mornin', Sheriff," Ben called.

"Mornin' yourself, Bill, I mean, Ben." Much of Wolf Creek, including the sheriff, still had not gotten used to calling Ben by his correct name, rather than Bill Torrance, the alias Ben had used when he rode into Wolf Creek. "I'd like you to meet…"

"Dave Benteen," Ben finished, sticking out his hand, which the gunsmith readily took. "Been quite some time since I've seen you, Dave. What've you been up to?"

"A little of this and that," Benteen said. "And a lot of travelin'. How about you, Ben?"

"The same," Ben answered. "Never expected to see you in this town. Then again, I never expected to be livin' in Kansas either. Seems like pretty much everyone lands in Wolf Creek sooner or later. You plannin' on stayin' long?"

Benteen shrugged. "*Quien sabe*?"

"You two know each other?" Satterlee questioned.

189

"Sure do," Ben answered. "Dave's the hombre who converted my Navies from cap and ball to .44 rimfire cartridge some time back. As you saw when the Danby gang ambushed us, that certainly makes for faster firin'. Saved my bacon more'n once. Either of you want some coffee? I just made a fresh pot."

"Not right now, thanks," Satterlee said. "I came by to ask if you'd reconsider my offer to become one of my deputies. You'd still be able to run your livery, and I'm certain the extra cash would come in handy. Ben, you're a natural for law enforcement. Don't tell me you haven't missed it since you left the Rangers."

"G.W., like I told you before, I appreciate the offer, but I just don't want anything more than my horses. Been burned too many times in the past."

Satterlee started to press the matter further, then let it drop. Clearly, whatever had driven Tolliver out of law work was something he didn't want to discuss, at least not yet. Satterlee looked at Tolliver's open shirt and changed the subject. He chuckled.

"Ben, too bad you don't want to become a deputy. That way when Edith Pettigrew files a complaint about you goin' around town half-naked, you could investigate it yourself and tell her you found no law about not wearin' a shirt in public in Wolf Creek."

Ben returned the sheriff's chuckle with one of his own.

"Figured Mrs. Pettigrew was tryin' to stir things up again. She came by here earlier with a gaggle of her church ladies."

190

"Ah, yes, the Wolf Creek Christian Ladies Quilting and Sewing Society," Satterlee said, with a sigh.

"Edith Pettigrew?" Benteen broke in.

"Edith Pettigrew, widow of Seth Pettigrew, one of the founders of Wolf Creek, and the town busybody, which is a polite way of sayin' she's a real pain in the butt," Satterlee explained. "Always findin' something to make a fuss about. Lately she's made it her business to complain every time she spots Ben not wearin' a shirt. Truthfully, I wonder whether she really enjoys seein' Ben shirtless."

"Yep, but I think she was disappointed today, G.W.," Ben said. "Had my shirt on and buttoned up tight when she and the rest of those squawking magpies showed up."

"So that's why she hasn't been by my office yet. Mebbe she went to see Marshal Gardner instead, or with luck won't bother either one of us, since she really doesn't have anything on you, this time."

"You didn't let me finish," Ben said. "Mrs. Pettigrew told me she had brought her friends along so they could see for themselves me paradin' on the streets half-naked. Said they intended to look into the matter. So, I told her if they wanted to look into the matter I'd oblige 'em. Pulled off my shirt and tossed it on the fence right in front of those women, then stood there like a Greek statue. You should've seen the looks on their faces. They ran off cacklin' like a bunch of wet hens."

"Oh, Lord, no," Satterlee said, with a groan. "Ben, you didn't."

"I sure enough did," Ben answered.

191

"That means Mrs. Pettigrew is either searchin' for me, or is in my office waitin' for my return," Satterlee said. "Reckon I might as well get back there and let her get her tirade over with."

"Sorry if I caused you more trouble, G.W.," Ben said.

"It don't matter," Satterlee answered. "If it wasn't you, Edith Pettigrew would find somethin' else to bother me with. Meantime, don't forget that deputy's job is open any time you want it."

"If I ever change my mind, you'll be the first to know," Ben said. "Dave, good seein' you again. Stop by first chance you get. We can catch up on old times."

"I'll do just that," Benteen promised. "Sheriff, if you don't mind my taggin' along a bit more, I'd kinda like to meet this Edith Pettigrew."

"It's your funeral," Satterlee said.

*\*\*\**

Cholla had disappeared into the barn while Ben talked with Satterlee and Benteen. Now he reappeared, his bridle, which he'd lifted from its peg, clamped in his teeth. He trotted up to Ben and tossed his head.

"You want to go for a ride, eh, pal?" Ben asked, as he took the bridle from Cholla. "Reckon that's not a bad idea. Work's all done until feedin' time anyhow."

Ben flipped the wooden sign on the big sliding door from "Open" to "Closed", took a piece of chalk from his shirt pocket and scrawled "Back after 4" under that, then, buttoning his shirt and tucking it in, headed inside the stable, Cholla at his heels. It only took a few minutes for him to put some jerky in his saddlebags, toss the saddle on

192

the big paint's back, slide the headstall over his ears and the bit into his mouth, and mount. Ten minutes later, the last buildings of Wolf Creek faded from sight.

Ben rode due west for several miles, letting Cholla choose his own pace, then turned northwest. He rode another mile, then turned his horse into the brush, following a barely discernible antelope trail. He kept on that trail for some distance, until he reached a jumble of boulders, most of which were horse-height and above. He weaved his way through those, the gaps getting ever narrower. The sure-footed Cholla, knowing their destination, never snorted a protest, just moved slowly but steadily onward, until they came to a sheer rock ledge, which rose at least seventy five feet straight up. The trail, what was left of it, turned left along the ledge's base. For three hundred yards, the trail ran along a knife-edged ridge top. To the right and left of the trail the ground dropped abruptly, a plunge of one hundred feet or more, until it returned to the base of the ledge on its right. To all appearances, there was no way over or around that ledge for a man on foot, let alone horseback, but Cholla turned sideways and sidled along the rocks, left hooves partially off the trail, until he came to a crack in the ledge. He walked half the length of his body, then stopped. Ben dismounted from the right and stepped into the defile. Cholla backed up and followed Ben. Man and horse squeezed their way through that narrow crack for two hundred yards, until it opened onto a small, steep-sided valley, surrounded on all sides by unscalable cliffs. Except for a little area directly below where Ben stood, the valley was filled by a deep, clear blue lake. Ben had discovered this geologic fluke of nature, which he'd named Blue Hole after the lake's color, his first time on the way to Wolf Creek. He had spied a roving band of Kiowa warriors before they managed to spot him. Traveling unarmed as usual, Ben's only hope for survival was to melt into the brush and find a hiding spot before being discovered. When he squeezed himself and his horse into that crevice, he'd never expected it to open onto this hidden little paradise. Bill doubted that anyone but himself, white or Indian, knew of its existence. There was certainly no sign any other human had ever trod here.

"We made it again, pard," Ben said to Cholla, tweaking his ears. "Neither of us better put on any pounds, though, or we'll never fit through that crack." He climbed back into the saddle and sent Cholla down the slope, the horse sliding most of the way on his haunches until they reached the bottom.

Ben dismounted and stripped the gear from Cholla, then peeled off his clothes. He pulled himself onto the paint's back and heeled Cholla into the cold, clear water. An eager swimmer, Cholla stuck his nose in the lake up to his eyes, blowing bubbles, then started pawing at the water before plunging in. Ben grabbed his horse's thick mane, wrapped his arms around Cholla's neck, and leaned low over the horse's withers as they struck out for the opposite shore, only Cholla's ears, eyes, and nostrils, and Ben's head and neck, visible above the surface. They made several trips across the lake and back before Cholla emerged from the water and shook himself vigorously, sending water droplets flying in all directions.

"Hey, take it easy, you," Ben chided. "I'm still up here, pretty much unprotected, and that smarts. Tryin' to get even just 'cause I had you gelded?"

Cholla merely snorted, then dropped his nose to graze.

"All right, all right. You're hungry," Ben said, then laughed. "Just occurred to me, Cholla. Imagine what Edith Pettigrew'd do if she saw me right now. Probably faint dead away. Course we don't have to worry about any woman findin' us here."

Ben sighed when a memory came flooding back. There had been a woman, one who he wished could be with him right now, and forever.

Cholla snorted again. Bill slid from his back and patted his shoulder.

"You go ahead and eat. I'm gonna snooze a bit before I grab a bite. We've got a couple of hours before we have to head back."

Ben found a spot where the grass was thickest and stretched out on his back, to allow the soft breeze and sunshine to dry him off.

*Sure wish G.W. would stop pesterin' me about becomin' a deputy,* he thought. *Of course, he's right about a couple of things. I'm good when it comes to bein' a lawman, and I love the work. But it's cost me too much, and I'm not talkin' about the bullets I've taken. The law cost me Madelaine, then Pete. It's not gonna take anyone else from me.*

A tear trickled down Ben's cheek. *Madelaine, the woman he'd loved more than life itself, even more than Cholla. Madelaine, the fiery Scots-Irish-French woman*

195

*he'd first met in San Antonio. Madelaine, with the emerald green eyes and blazing red hair, who had loved him with a passion as intense as that flaming hair, a love which he had returned with just as much passion. Madelaine, who had indeed seen him naked and swimming Cholla bareback across a lake… and who, when they returned, ripped off her own clothes and jumped up behind Ben, joining him as Cholla plunged back into the lake, her arms around Ben's waist and her full breasts pushed up against his back, clinging to him atop the powerfully swimming horse. Madelaine, who loved him without question… until he remained out on a Ranger patrol just a few days too long, and returned to find her gone.*

"Never thought I could even look at another woman after Madelaine," Ben murmured. "Then, when I finally do think I might be able to love a woman again, that bastard Jim Danby took Anne from me. Well, there's two things I know for certain. I'm never gonna love a woman again, and I'm never gonna pin on a badge again, neither."

Ben rolled onto his stomach, cradled his head in his arms, and caressed by the warm breeze, soft as a woman's touch, although he'd never admit that, drifted off to sleep.

\*\*\*

"Gonna be a good day, Cholla," Ben said, early in the morning several days later. He had just rolled the last wheelbarrow-load of manure and soiled bedding out of the stable and dumped it on the pile out back. "I'll get your brushes. Time to clean you up nice and shiny. Head back inside. I'll be with you in a minute."

He sent the big paint back into the barn with a gentle slap on the rump.

"Mr. Tolliver! I need to speak with you, right now!"

"At least it *was* gonna be a good day," Ben muttered as Reverend Dill Hyder, pastor of the nearby Mount Pisgah Methodist Church, came hurrying up to the back of the stable. "Last thing I needed was that Bible-thumper complainin' again."

Dill Hyder was a Massachusetts transplant, and had been a rabid abolitionist before the War. He carried himself with an air of haughty arrogance, not unlike how the Pharisees of Israel must have appeared, Ben often thought. The minister wore his hair slicked back, which only emphasized his thin, bony face, a face accentuated by an extremely long, narrow nose. More than one person in Wolf Creek had described Hyder as "horse-faced", although never in his presence, of course. And Ben would certainly never have insulted any of his equine friends by comparing them to Hyder. Ben thought Hyder much more closely resembled the picture of a moose he had once seen. How the minister, who was in his early forties, had managed to convince the much younger and quite attractive Kathleen McCain, Derrick's younger sister, to marry him was a mystery to just about everyone in Wolf Creek. Their marriage did not seem to be a happy one.

"Good morning to you, Reverend," Ben called back.

"It certainly is not a good morning," Hyder answered. "The wind is out of the north again, which

197

means it is blowing the odors from your stable, and its attendant manure pile, right into my church."

"Thought the church was God's, not any one man's, Reverend," Ben retorted. He always had a hard time concealing his distaste for this self-important sky pilot.

"Don't get uppity with me!" Hyder answered. "My congregation should not have to put up with that smell. I've asked you before, and I ask you again, what do you intend to do about it?"

"Short of askin' the Good Lord to have the wind blow in the opposite direction, or waitin' until September or October when the weather cools down, there ain't a whole lot I can do about it," Ben answered. "Besides, it ain't all that bad. Can't figure why it bothers you so much. Last I heard there were plenty of horses in Massachusetts, too… or does manure from Northern horses smell like honeysuckle and rose petals?"

"Your stable and its odors are keeping me from doing God's work!" Hyder was shouting now, as if giving one of his fire and brimstone sermons. His face was flushed. "Some of my people leave services before they conclude, rather than putting up with the stench."

"Then I'd imagine some of Jesus's followers left His sermons early also," Ben replied.

"What do you mean by that?"

"Well, I figure it this way. Jesus and His apostles tramped all over the burnin' hot desert, wearin' heavy robes, usually barefoot or with just sandals on their feet. Doesn't seem to me they had the chance to take a bath all that often. I'd imagine they smelled pretty bad most days."

"That is blasphemy!"

"I hardly think so, Reverend. I don't believe most folks were all that concerned about how Jesus looked or smelled, but were mostly interested in what He had to say. Don't forget, Jesus Himself said not to judge a man by his appearance, but what is in his heart."

"Don't try and debate theology with me, Mr. Tolliver," Hyder thundered. "You don't even come to church on Sunday. You are a godless heathen!"

"No, Reverend, I am a Christian, as are you," Ben said. "However, unlike you, I don't believe God condemns almost everyone to Hell for the slightest transgression. The God I learned about in Sunday school is a God of love, as is Jesus, His only-begotten Son. I believe in a kind and merciful God, full of love and forgiveness, not some vengeful God always ready to smite down the people He created and loves. I'd imagine your Hellfire and damnation sermons drive far more people out of your church before services are over than the smell of horse manure. In fact, mebbe it's the smell of all that sulfur and blazin' brimstone drivin' 'em away. As far as me not goin' to church, I've always found myself closer to God while I'm on the back of a horse, out enjoyin' and appreciatin' all the wonders of God's handiwork. I don't need any two-bit preacher to tell me how great God is, or that He loves and cares for all creation. That's not sayin' if the right preacher comes along I wouldn't start goin' to church come Sunday mornings. It's just that you and Reverend Stone, both so quick to condemn folks, well, neither of you sure ain't the right one."

Hyder swallowed hard, trying to keep his temper in check.

"Clearly there is no point in continuing this conversation," he said. "It's obvious you have no intention of addressing this problem. However, this is not the end of the matter. I'll be speaking to Mayor Henry at the first opportunity."

"While frequenting his establishment?" Ben asked, eyes wide with innocence.

"How dare you imply… You are clearly going to Hell," Hyder said, his voice tight.

"I sure hope not, Reverend. But that's up to the Lord, not you. In the meantime, if you're so worried about my immortal soul, you might try prayin' for it, rather'n sendin' me to Hell on your own. Now, as you said about your work, you're keeping me from mine… good, honest work which the Lord has provided. And let me remind you, Jesus was born in a stable, perhaps one not much different from this one. I'd imagine there was even a manure pile out back. Have a nice day, Reverend."

Ben went back inside his barn, leaving Hyder staring at his back. Cholla popped his head up from where he was nibbling on some loose hay and whickered.

"You're right, pard. Day can't get any worse after arguin' with that sanctimonious son of a bitch."

Ben was about to find out just how wrong he was.

\*\*\*

Ben had finished grooming Cholla and was in his office, going over his ledgers, when he heard his horse snort from his stall, then whinny shrilly.

"I'm busy, pard," he shouted. "Just relax. If I don't figure out some way to bring in a bit more business, neither one of us'll eat next month. We'd better hope another trail herd hits town, and soon."

"Mr. Tolliver, where are you?"

"Oh, no." Ben put his head in his hands and groaned. Just who he didn't need, Edith Pettigrew.

"Mr. Tolliver," she called again, more loudly.

"I'm back here in my office, Mrs. Pettigrew," Ben answered. "Be with you in a minute."

He slammed the book shut. No point in putting off the inevitable. However, before leaving the office, he made sure his shirt was buttoned up tight.

To Ben's surprise, when he went into the aisle he found Edith Pettigrew stroking Cholla's nose. His horse was nickering softly with pleasure.

"Good morning, Mrs. Pettigrew. What can I do for you?"

The widow woman ran her gaze up and down Ben before replying.

"Good morning, Mr. Tolliver. I'm not here for the reason you think. This visit is strictly business. I would like to purchase a horse and buggy."

"A horse and buggy?" Ben echoed.

"Yes. Perhaps I should explain. When my dear Seth, may the Lord rest his soul, was alive, we owned some of the finest horses and carriages in Wolf Creek. Seth taught me how to drive, even how to harness, and I am quite good at it, if I do say so myself."

"I see," Ben said. "Then why did you sell your horses, if I may ask."

"It seemed like the thing to do at the time. Without Seth, I just didn't enjoy long drives in the country. Then, later, money became an issue. I'm not as wealthy as most people in Wolf Creek think... at least I wasn't."

"Mebbe you'd better clarify that."

"Perhaps I should. I received word recently that I've come into a rather large inheritance. My Aunt Marie passed away a short time ago. She was married to a man who made a small fortune selling supplies to the miners in California. He was killed in a landslide out there, and naturally all his money went to her. Since they never had any children, and I am my aunt's only survivor, I am the sole beneficiary of her estate. I realize it's impolite to talk about money, very gauche, don't you think, Mr. Tolliver?"

"I reckon," Ben said, with a shrug.

"Anyway, just so you know I am serious about this purchase, my inheritance is well into six figures. I can show you a letter from the attorney handling my late aunt's affairs if you wish. Most of the money will be kept in trust in St. Louis, but a good piece of it will be in my account at the Wolf Creek Savings and Loan within the week."

"That won't be necessary, Mrs. Pettigrew. I'm certain you're a thoroughly honest woman."

"Of course I am. Also, naturally I would keep any animal I might purchase here at your stable, Mr. Tolliver. That would be simpler than having to hire a stableman to care for a horse at my home. Would that be satisfactory?"

"I'm certain we could work something out," Ben said, not quite sure of what to make of this conversation.

"Fine, fine," Mrs. Pettigrew said. "Do you have anything which might be suitable for me?"

"I believe so, yes," Ben answered. "I have a nice gray mare here, quite young, about five years old. She's spirited, but very willing and obedient. Dr. Munro was supposed to purchase her, but changed his mind. I'm afraid the good doctor doesn't take to horses as well as he does people. There's also a fine buggy which was supposed to be part of the deal. If you like both, I can offer you a good price."

"I'm not one to haggle," Mrs. Pettigrew answered. "If I like the mare, I'm certain any price you set will be fair. Would I be able to see her now?"

"Of course," Ben said. "She's in the back corral. The buggy is parked next to that, so you can see both at the same time. Just follow me."

With Cholla at their heels, Ben and Mrs. Pettigrew headed for the corral. Inside the enclosure was a leggy dapple-gray mare. She was trotting along the fence, head high, but stopped at Ben's whistle and walked up to him, allowing him to scratch her ears.

"Here she is. Her name's Josie," Ben said. "What do you think?"

"She certainly is a fine-looking animal," Mrs. Pettigrew said. "When can I try her out?"

"Right now, if you'd like. I'll harness her up. Aren't you worried about what people will say though, you being alone with me in a buggy?"

"Not one bit. Everyone knows I am a completely respectable woman. Now, if you would get the mare ready, that would be lovely."

It only took Ben a few minutes to hitch up the mare. He helped Mrs. Pettigrew into the buggy's seat, but she stopped him when he started to climb up next to her.

"Mr. Tolliver, where are your guns?"

"I believe you know I don't like wearing guns, Mrs. Pettigrew," Ben answered. "They're safely put away."

"Yes, but after the Danby gang's attack, and with those awful Kiowas still roaming about, I would feel much safer if you wore your weapons," Mrs. Pettigrew replied. "Would it be too much trouble?"

"I guess not," Ben said, with a shrug. "Be right back."

He headed back into the barn to retrieve his Colts.

"That's much better," Mrs. Pettigrew said when Ben returned, climbed into the buggy, and picked up the reins. His guns now hung at his hips. "Let's go. It's a lovely day for a ride."

Ben clucked to Josie and slapped the reins lightly on her rump. With Cholla following, he held the mare to a walk for half-a-mile, until she warmed up, then pushed her into a trot. She moved out willingly, clearly a horse who wanted to please.

"She's wonderful!" Mrs. Pettigrew exclaimed. She edged closer to Ben. "It's clear you know your horseflesh, Mr. Tolliver."

"I just like horses, that's all, ma'am."

"Please, call me Edith. I insist. Ma'am sounds so formal… and old."

"All right." Ben slid away from her.

"May I call you Ben?" she asked, sliding closer and leaning against him.

"I guess that'll be all right," Ben answered. "Would you like to take the reins?"

"Could I?"

"She's going to be your horse, so you might as well give her a try."

"Wonderful." Mrs. Pettigrew took the reins and urged Josie into an extended trot. She kept the mare at that pace for two more miles, slowed her to a trot for another mile, then walked her for a mile still. At that point, she turned the rig to the right, off the trail, and pulled to a stop behind a grove of cottonwoods and willows.

"Why are we stopping, Mrs. Pettigrew, I mean, Edith?" Ben asked.

"I'm feeling a bit faint," she answered. "It must be the exhilaration from our drive. Josie is every bit the horse you said she is, and more. I just need to rest a moment and catch my breath. Perhaps you would be kind enough to wet my handkerchief in that creek, so I can dab it on my face to cool off."

"Of course," Ben said. "Let me help you down." He secured the reins, then stepped out of the buggy and went to the opposite side. When he attempted to assist Mrs. Pettigrew down, she fell, leaning against Ben for a moment longer than necessary.

"I apologize, Ben," she said.

"No apology necessary. You just slipped, that's all," Ben answered. "Let me have your handkerchief."

"Of course." She removed the cloth from her reticule and handed it to him. By the time Ben returned from the creek, she had unbuttoned the top two buttons of her blouse, revealing a good portion of her breasts, still round and firm.

"Here's your handkerchief."

"Thank you, Ben." She took the lace cloth, dabbed it at her face, then her cleavage.

"It's much warmer than I expected," she said, undoing yet another button.

"Have you decided on Josie yet?" Ben asked, growing uncomfortable.

"She's a fine horse, but I was thinking along the lines of something a bit more powerful, in case I ran into trouble on the prairie. A big stallion, perhaps."

"I'm sorry, Edith. I don't keep any stallions in my stock. Unless you're breeding horses, a stud horse is nothing but trouble. Heck, I even had my Cholla gelded. And a horse like Josie can outrun almost any pursuers. I think maybe we should start back."

"Not quite yet," she said. "Ben, don't you find me attractive? Most men would."

Ben hesitated a moment before answering. Despite her age, at least twenty years older than him, Edith Pettigrew was still a fairly handsome woman. She had lost some weight, no doubt at least partially due to her opium habit. The loss of pounds revealed curves which had heretofore been hidden, at least as long as Ben had lived in Wolf Creek. There were slight wrinkles around her eyes, signs of dissipation from her addiction, but today those eyes were clear. She hadn't gotten into her opium, at least not yet.

"You are a good-looking woman, yes," Ben answered. "I'm sure you'll find the right man some day, and get married again."

"Perhaps," she said. "But I have needs now, Ben, just like any woman. I'm sure you must have needs also."

"Those feelings have long been buried," Ben answered.

"I can make them come alive again," she said. "It's been far too long since I've been with a man. In fact, since my dear Seth passed on."

"Mrs. Pettigrew…"

"Edith."

"All right, Edith. I think we should end this, right here and now. You have your reputation to think of, and I can't ever love another woman."

"No one will know," she answered. "As far as love, I'm not worried about that. I need you, Ben Tolliver. I've needed you since that day the Danby gang attacked Wolf Creek."

She stepped closer, wrapped her arms around Ben's neck, and kissed him firmly on the mouth, so hard she crushed his lips, drawing blood.

"Don't tell me you don't need a woman too," she whispered. She slipped a hand inside his shirt, rubbing his chest. Before Ben could even utter a protest, she had his shirt open and pulled off. She ran her hand over his belly, then inside his pants. Despite himself, Ben groaned as his body responded. He slid her blouse off her shoulders and began kissing her cleavage.

"Just a minute, Ben." Mrs. Edith Pettigrew, the self-proclaimed moral compass of Wolf Creek, unbuckled his gunbelt, tossed it aside, then unbuttoned Ben's pants and let them drop to his ankles. With amazing efficiency, she then removed her skirt, petticoat, and stockings and let them fall.

"Now."

Locked in each other's arms, they sank to the grass. Neither had any illusions about this relationship. There was no love involved here, just the passions of two people who had been far too long without being with a member of the opposite sex. They made love hard and fast, completely spent by the time they were finished.

"Thank you, Ben."

"We shouldn't have…" Ben began, then was interrupted by a whinny from Cholla as three young Chinese men emerged from the trees.

"Very nice. Very nice, fine lady. You are indeed ready for the Jade Chamber," one said.

"What the…?" Ben attempted to scramble to his feet, hampered by his pants still wrapped around his ankles.

Mrs. Pettigrew screamed. She also rose, attempting to cover herself with her hands.

"What is the meaning of this?" she demanded.

"My uncle sent us to collect your debt. You will recall your promise that, if you were unable to pay for your 'medical supplies', you would work off your debt in the Jade Chamber. A lady of such status will be a great addition."

"I'm not going anywhere with you. I told Tsu Chiao he would have his money next week."

"He has decided not to wait any longer. You will come with us, now."

"The lady ain't goin' anywhere," Ben said. At that two of the Chinese pulled out pistols, heavy old Dragoon Colts.

"Do not interfere and you will not be harmed."

"I'm not lettin' you take the lady," Ben repeated. When he started to edge toward his gunbelt, the third Chinese pulled a long, curved sword from his belt and placed the blade alongside Ben's genitals.

"If you try and stop us, I will remove your manhood like so, *chop chop*," he warned.

"Ben, don't try anything," Mrs. Pettigrew pleaded. "They'll kill you if you do."

"You do anything to hurt her and Tsu Chiao will answer to me," Ben said.

"She will not be harmed."

"I'll hold you to that," Ben said. He was seething inside, helpless against the guns being held on him. He also knew those men had no intention of leaving him alive. One thing was for certain, though. He sure wasn't gonna die without a fight, with his pants down out here in the brush. He just had to await his chance.

"We've wasted enough time, Mrs. Pettigrew," the leader ordered. "Get dressed and let's go."

"All right. But may I get my purse first? I need my handkerchief."

"Of course."

"Thank you."

Mrs. Pettigrew picked up her beaded reticule from where she had dropped it, reached inside, pulled out a two-shot Derringer, and shot the nearest Chinese in the chest. He stumbled back, blood spurting from the close-range wound.

The other two men, stunned at the sudden turn of events, turned their attention away from Ben. They were too slow to react as he dove for his gunbelt and yanked out one of his Colts. He shot the man closest to Mrs. Pettigrew in the back, not giving him the time to kill her, then shot the swordsman three times in the belly. The man buckled, eyes glazing, and crumpled to the dirt. Ben came to his feet.

"Edith, are you all right?" he asked.

"I… I think so. Are they all dead?"

Ben quickly checked the bodies. The gut-shot Chinese was just breathing his last. "They sure are."

"That means I… I killed a man."

"You had no choice. You saved both our lives. Now listen to me. Can you take Josie and head back to town?"

"I… believe so. She didn't run off?"

"No. I trained her to accept gunfire, so she's right there where we left her. I want you to get dressed, climb back in that buggy, and head for town like nothing has happened."

"But… what about those men?"

"I'll take care of them. Remember, nothing happened out here. Get dressed and get back to town. When you reach my stable, find Dickie Dildine, tell him you just bought Josie, and have him take care of her. He'll put her up and put the rig away. Tell him I'll be back

210

shortly, that I had some business to attend to. No more than that."

"All right."

Ben and Mrs. Pettigrew hurriedly redressed.

"Don't forget what I said. Nothing happened out here." Ben repeated his warning as he helped her back into the buggy. "You drive into town all calm and happy, like a woman who has just been for a long buggy ride and purchased a fine rig would act. Can you do that?"

"I must, so I will. You can depend on me."

"Good. One other thing," Ben said.

"What's that?"

"Tomorrow, you might want to see Dr. Munro and ask him to help you get off the opium," Ben said. "Things will only get worse for you unless you do."

"I don't take opium," Mrs. Pettegrew snapped.

"I'm sorry, but it's an open secret in Wolf Creek that you like your 'medicine'," Ben answered. "Tsu Chiao will only get his hooks deeper into you if you don't quit. Now get goin'."

He slapped Josie on the rump, putting her into a trot. Once Mrs. Pettigrew was out of sight, he found one of the Chinese's horses, removed its saddle and bridle and transferred those to Cholla.

"No lariat, so we'd better hope one of these 'nephews' of Tsu Chiao had some rope in his saddlebags, Cholla," Ben said.

Ben checked the gear from all three horses, cursing to himself when he found no rope.

211

"Reckon I'll have to use their reins. Gotta scatter these mounts anyway. They sure won't go where I've gotta go."

Ben stripped the gear from all three horses and chased them into the brush. Sooner or later they would find their way back to Wolf Creek. He took the reins from the bridles and used those as ropes, using the longest piece to tie one man by the wrists to his saddlehorn, then tied the other two wrist to ankle to the first man. Finally, he tied the two remaining saddles, blankets, and what was left of the bridles to the last body.

"Let's go, Cholla," Ben ordered, as he swung into the saddle. "Gotta put these hombres where no one'll ever find them."

With the three dead Chinese dragging behind, Ben stuck to the brush, heading for Blue Hole. Having to avoid the main trail took extra time, so it was mid-afternoon before he reached the sheer rock ledge.

"No way to get these three through that crevice, Cholla," Ben said. "Reckon I'll toss 'em over right here."

Ben dismounted, slashed the reins binding the dead men, and shoved the bodies over the cliff, along with their gear. He took the borrowed saddle and bridle off Cholla and tossed those over the edge, also.

"That takes care of 'em. Cover our trail, and no one'll ever find 'em," Ben said to Cholla. "Looks like it may rain later tonight. That'll help wash away any sign too."

Ben climbed onto Cholla's back and put him into a trot. "Y'know, horse," he said. "You could've saved me a lot of trouble if you'd been payin' attention and let me

212

know sooner those Chinese were sneakin' up. Guess you were too busy nuzzlin' up to Josie." Cholla snorted. "Yeah, you're right, pard. I wasn't exactly keepin' my eyes open either. You think mebbe Edith Pettigrew set me up? Wonder if she knew Tsu Chiao had sent his men after her, and hoped things would turn out just the way they did? Reckon that's why she made sure I wore my guns? We might just have to try and find out. We'd also better hope she keeps her mouth shut, even though it was self-defense. Smarter thing would have been to take the bodies back to town and tell the sheriff just that, but that'd only make more trouble. Better to keep Tsu Chiao guessin' as to what happened."

Ben knew how to cover a track as well as any Comanche, and he did just than on the way back to the ambush site. By the time he completely erased all hoof prints and buggy tracks there, he left no sign anyone had ever been at that grove. He checked the area one last time, then hit the main road and put Cholla into a long-reaching lope. They pulled up in front of Ben's stable an hour before sunset. Dickie Dildine was seated on a barrel out front, waiting for them.

"Ben. There you are," he said.

"Howdy, Dickie. You see Mrs. Pettigrew?"

"Yeah, I seen her."

"She tell you she bought Josie?"

"Yeah. Yeah, she did that."

Ben knew he had to be patient with the mentally challenged man, or Dickie would clam up and not say a word for two days.

"Did you feed and groom Josie for her?"

"Yeah. Yeah. Cleaned the buggy and put it away, too."

"What about Mrs. Pettigrew?"

"Mrs. Pettigrew? She's a fine lady. Always gives me a dollar when I fetch her medicine."

"But what about this afternoon?"

"This afternoon? Oh, yeah. She gave me two dollars for takin' care of Josie. Two whole dollars."

"Two dollars? That's great, Dickie. She gone home?"

"I guess. You want some help with Cholla?"

"No, but I'm obliged, Dickie. You can head on home."

"All right, Ben. Oh, wait, I forgot. There's one other thing."

"What's that, Dickie?"

"Lemme think. Oh yeah. Deputy Croy's been lookin' all over for you. Says if I see you I should tell you to find him right quick."

"Deputy Croy?"

"Yeah, Deputy Croy."

"All right, Dickie. I'll head for the marshal's office and see if I can find Quint."

"You want me to watch the barn until you come back?"

"No, you've been a big help already. Just head on home, and I'll see you tomorrow."

"All right, Ben."

Ben waited until Dickie left, then pulled off his gunbelt and tossed it inside the stable before heading into town. *Wonder what Quint Croy wants me for,* Ben thought, as he walked an exhausted Cholla down North Street. He could think of only one thing. Edith Pettigrew must have let slip what had happened earlier that day.

***

Just about everyone in Wolf Creek was used to seeing Ben ride his big paint saddleless and bridleless, so no one gave him a second glance as he rode along South Street toward the marshal's office. Quint Croy met him about two blocks from the place.

"Ben. 'Bout time you showed up. I've been turnin' the town upside down tryin' to find you. Dickie Dildine tell you that?"

"Yeah, Quint, he said you wanted to see me, pronto. What's this all about?"

"You'll find out in a couple of minutes, soon as we reach the office. Meantime, you should probably know that Edith Pettigrew stopped by to see Marshal Gardner a little bit ago. Her usual complaint. She spotted you not wearin' a shirt again."

"I've gotta plead guilty as charged." Ben said, with a chuckle. Edith Pettigrew had just a short while ago seen him wearing much less than a shirt. He also sighed with relief. So far, she had kept quiet about the ambush, and had even been clever enough to come up with a small ruse. "You gonna lock me up?"

"Nah," Quint replied, with a chuckle of his own. "If I did, that woman would only be hangin' around your cell window, tryin' to see if you were wearin' your shirt, or more likely hopin' you weren't. Well, here we are."

They nosed their horses to the rail and dismounted, Quint looping his dun's reins over it. Cholla would stand

215

there untied for hours if need be, patiently awaiting Ben's return.

Two people were waiting in the office when they stepped inside. One was a man in his late fifties, who had thick burnsides framing a florid face, and dark hair carefully pomaded in place. He was dressed in an expensive business suit. Ben stopped in his tracks at sight of the second. That was a boy, about eight years old. The youngster had flaming red hair, light green eyes the color of jade, and a smattering of freckles across his nose.

"Sorry it took me so long to find Ben, Mr. Higginbotham," Quint said. "Finally tracked him down."

"That's quite all right, Deputy," Higginbotham said. "Mr. Tolliver, allow me to introduce myself. I am Phineas T. Higginbotham, of the law firm of Dowd, Higginbotham, Bedard, and Bove of Austin, Texas. We have had quite the time trying to locate you, sir. This young man with me is Daniel... Daniel Tolliver, your son."

"My... son?" Ben repeated. The boy clearly was the image of Madelaine, but Ben's son?

"Yes, your son," Higginbotham said. "This letter will explain." He removed a folded sheet of paper from his inside jacket pocket, unfolded it, and handed it to Ben. It carried the letterhead of Higginbotham's firm.

*Mr. Tolliver,*

*Eight years ago, you were informed that your wife, Madelaine Colraine Tolliver, had died in childbirth, and that the child was stillborn. The truth of the matter is the child, a boy, survived, and your wife's last wish was that he be placed in you, his father's, care to be raised.*

*However, Madelaine's parents and sister felt that you, as an itinerant horse wrangler and sometime Texas Ranger, would not have been a suitable parent for the child. Therefore, the decision was made to tell you both mother and son  had died. The infant was removed to the Colraine's home in San Antonio before you were informed of your wife's untimely passing. He was with them until five months ago, when both were taken by cholera. The same illness also claimed Natalie, Madelaine's sister. The only surviving Colraines, a niece and two nephews, have no interest in raising a child not their own. Therefore, the family retained our firm to locate you and remand Daniel James Tolliver to your custody and care. Once you agree and sign the necessary papers, you will have full custody of your son.*

The letter was signed by Phineas T. Higginbotham, for the firm.

"My son," Ben said yet again. He looked at the boy, who gave him a shy grin.

"Yes," Higginbotham said. "I have the papers right here. All you need do is sign them. If you don't, then Daniel will be placed in a San Antonio orphanage."

"We sure can't have that," Ben said. "Quint, you got a pen and ink?"

Quint pointed to a pen and inkwell on Sam Gardner's desk.

"Been sittin' there waitin' for you."

"How about it, son?" Ben asked the boy. "Looks like you and me've got a lot of gettin' acquainted ahead. You want to live in Kansas?"

217

"I reckon," Daniel said, with a shrug.

"Good."

Ben and Higginbotham signed the papers, with Quint Croy as witness. The deputy had a smile a mile wide across his face when they finished.

"Ben, you don't know how hard it was keepin' quiet until I got you in the office," he said. "Congratulations, pardner. Looks like you've got a fine boy there."

"If he's anything at all like his ma, he sure is," Ben said. "Mr. Higginbotham, I thank you for everything, especially for your hard work in tracking me down."

"All part of the job," Higginbotham said.

"Nevertheless, I'm obliged," Ben answered. "Can I buy you supper for your trouble?"

"Thank you, but no," Higginbotham answered. "I have to meet a, um, client at Abby Potter's Boarding House. Then I'll be catching the next outbound train."

"I understand," Ben said. "How about you, Danny? Or do you prefer Dan? I'll bet you're hungry. When'd you eat last?"

"Danny."

"I got him a bite at Joe's Whistlestop when we got off the train," Higginbotham said. "However, that was several hours ago."

"Then we'd better head for Ma's," Ben said. "C'mon, Danny."

The boy picked up a small carpetbag as Ben opened the door and stepped outside. Cholla nickered a greeting.

"This here's Cholla, my horse," Ben said. "Cholla, this is Danny."

218

Cholla nuzzled Danny's chest. Danny patted the big paint's nose.

"I see you two'll get along just fine," Ben said. "Danny, step over here and I'll put you on Cholla."

Ben lifted the boy onto Cholla's back, then climbed up behind him. Ma's Café was diagonally across Fourth Street from the marshal's office, so it was only a moment before they reached the restaurant, headed inside, and settled at a corner table.

"Ben! Who have you got with you?" "Ma" Adams, the proprietor, fairly shouted.

"This is Danny, my son," Ben answered.

"Your son? He gonna be visitin' for a spell?"

"He's gonna be stayin' with me permanently," Ben said.

"He is? Well, Danny, you're a lucky boy to have Ben for a dad. How about some vittles. You hungry?"

"I sure am, Ma'am," Danny said.

"Then a big bowl of my beef stew and some homemade bread will fill you right up," Ma said. "Bet I can scare up a glass of milk and a nice chunk of apple pie, too. Same for you, Ben?"

"That'll be fine, Ma."

While they were waiting for their meal, Clay Dillard, the Wolf Creek stationmaster for the Atchison, Topeka, and Santa Fe, stopped in for his usual supper.

"Ben. See that lawyer fella found you," he said. "So this is your boy?"

"Word spreads fast, Clay," Ben answered. "Yeah, this is Danny."

219

"Good to meet you, boy," Dillard said. "Mebbe you'll be just what Ben needs. Ben, good luck to you both."

"Thanks, Clay."

\*\*\*

After supper, Ben took Danny home to his stable.

"You want to help me with the horses, Danny, or just watch?" he asked.

"Dunno," Danny said.

"Tell you what then. You just watch for tonight, then decide what you'd like to do to help when you can," Ben said. "All right?"

"All right."

After caring for the horses, Ben, with Danny in tow, headed for the small room that served as his living quarters.

"Time to hit the sack, Danny," Bed said. "We'll both have to squeeze into the same bed tonight. Tomorrow, we'll go to Pratt's Mercantile to buy you your own bed. After that we'll stop at Birdie's General Store to get you some good boots and a proper hat. How's that sound?"

"All right," Danny said. He looked up at Ben with wide eyes.

"Mr. Tolliver, sir?"

"Whoa, none of that. I'm your father."

"That's what I want to ask. Are you really my pa?"

Ben grabbed the boy and squeezed him in a bear hug.

"I sure am, Danny. And you don't ever have to worry about that again, you understand. In fact, I'm also

220

gonna have to buy you a horse, so I can teach you to ride. Can't have a boy of mine not knowin' how to ride a bronc, can we?"

"No, I guess not… pa," Danny said, smiling, but with tears rolling down his cheeks.

"Good, that's settled. Now get into bed. Been a long day, and we both need our shut-eye."

Ben lay next to Danny, gazing at the boy for quite some time after Danny had fallen asleep.

*A son,* he thought. *This changes everything. Got to make sure my boy's got a future in Wolf Creek. That means makin' sure it's a safe place for him to grow up. Guess I'll be strappin' on my guns again. And first chance I get I'm gonna tell Sheriff Satterlee I'll take that deputy's job.*

Of course, there was the small matter of Tsu Chiao's three dead "nephews." Ben pushed that thought out of his mind. Right now, his only concern was Danny. He fell asleep with his arm wrapped protectively around his son.

THE END

## ABOUT THE AUTHORS:

### JAMES J.GRIFFIN

I've had a great interest in the West and particularly Texas Rangers from when I was a kid, so it was natural when I started writing the Rangers would be the subject of my novels. Over the years I've accumulated enough knowledge about the Rangers to be considered an amateur historian of the organization. I also amassed a large collection of Texas Ranger artifacts, which are now in the permanent collections of the Texas Ranger Hall of Fame and Museum in Waco. Currently, I am in the midst of writing a ten issue series of short stories for High Noon Press. These are ebooks, titled A Ranger Named Rowdy, A Texas Ranger Tim Bannon story. The first four are already available, with six more to follow.

My other great passion in life is horses, especially Paints. I've owned horses most of my life, and currently own an American Paint Horse named Yankee. He is a Pet Partners certified therapy animal, and we make visits to local hospitals and nursing homes. In addition, Yank and I are members of the Connecticut Horse Council Volunteer Horse Patrol. We act as auxiliary park rangers, patrolling state parks and forests.

I'm a native New Englander, and as much as I love the West I love New England, particularly my adopted home state of New Hampshire, even more. Currently, I divide my time between Branford, Connecticut and Keene, New Hampshire.

To learn more about my books, and see some of Yankee's tricks, check out my website at www.jamesjgriffin.net .

**JERRY GUIN**
I'm happy as heck to be included in this anthology. "Asa Pepper's Place," was a challenge that I could not resist. Since writing the first chapter of *Wolf Creek 3: Murder in Dogleg City* last year, I've had some other new publications:

In April, "Justified" –a short story in eBook form –was published by High Noon Press.
On June 15, La Frontera released *Dead or Alive,* an anthology which includes my story "Who Shot Billy Dean." Coming soon: "Charlie's Money," a novella in eBook from High Noon Press; my novel *Drover's Bounty*, a Black Horse Western from Robert Hale, has a release date of August 30th. All are available at Amazon under Jerry Guin or J.L. Guin.

**CLAY MORE**
Clay More is actually my western pen name. My real name is Keith Souter and I live in England within arrow-shot of the ruins of a medieval castle, the scene of two of my historical novels. I am a part time doctor, medical journalist and novelist, writing in four different genres - crime, historical, YA and westerns. I also enjoy the

challenge of short fiction for which I have won a couple of prizes, including a 2006 Fish Award for my story *The Villain's Tale*.

My medical background finds its way into a lot of my writing, as can be seen in most of my western novels. My character in Wolf Creek is Doctor Logan Munro, the town doctor, who is gradually revealing more about himself with each book he appears in. Another of my characters is Doctor Marcus Quigley, dentist, gambler and bounty hunter who is appearing as a monthly eBook short story, published by High Noon Press. I am a member of various writers' organisations, including Western Fictioneers and Western Writers of America. If you care to find out more about me, visit my website: http://www.keithsouter.co.uk

**JACQUIE ROGERS**
I'm a country girl at heart, raised on a dairy farm in Idaho — a great place to grow up. My friend and I rode our horses all over the Owyhee Mountains and managed to get ourselves in just about every sort of pickle. We fought outlaws all over Graveyard Point and won every time. Now I live in the suburbs of Seattle with my husband who is also my cheerleader (sans pompoms) and proofreader. I write in several genres including fantasy romance, and YA fantasy, but mostly western historical romance. The fourth book in my award-winning Hearts of Owyhee series will be released later this year. The first three titles are Much Ado About Marshals, Much Ado About Madams, and Much Ado About Mavericks. Judge Not is the first installment of The Muleskinner series of short stories, and

as well as my debut foray into wild world of traditional westerns, which are my first love.

I love to hear from readers! Please visit my website, http://www.JacquieRogers.com or join the fun at Facebook, http://www.facebook.com/JacquieRogersAuthor. I also wrangle the popular western blog, Romancing The West, http://romancingthewest.blogspot.com, and the Western Historical Romance Book Club on Facebook, http://www.facebook.com/groups/WHRbookclub.

**CHERYL PIERSON**
A native Oklahoman, I live in Oklahoma City and write historical westerns and western romance. My Wolf Creek character, Derrick McCain, who is featured in "It Takes a Man," is also included in *WC Book 1: Bloody Trail,* and *WC Book 5: Showdown at Demon's Drop.* Look for more about Derrick and his half-brother, Carson Ridge, in the exciting WC Christmas anthology coming this fall, and thanks for dropping in on the citizens of Wolf Creek!

My short story, "The Keepers of Camelot," included in the Western Fictioneers' Christmas anthology *Six Guns and Slay Bells: A Creepy Cowboy Christmas*, was nominated for the 2013 Western Fictioneers Peacemaker Award in the short story category. I also have a new release, *Kane's Chance*, that will appeal to all ages. It's a coming-of-age story of a young boy in the old west, a novel you won't want to miss.

Right now, my website is under construction, but you can click here for a listing of all my work:
***Cheryl's Amazon Author Page:***
*https://www.amazon.com/author/cherylpierson*

## TROY D. SMITH

I am from the Upper Cumberland region of Tennessee. My work has appeared in many anthologies, and in journals such as *Louis L'Amour Western Magazine, Civil War Times,* and *Wild West.* In addition, I've written novels in several genres—from mysteries like *Cross Road Blues* to the Civil War epic *Good Rebel Soil.* My other Civil War epic, *Bound for the Promise-Land,* won a Spur Award in 2001 and I was a finalist on two other occasions. I've been a finalist for the Peacemaker Award three times, winning once for best short story, and am currently serving as president of Western Fictioneers. I received my Ph.D. from the University of Illinois, and teach American Indian history at Tennessee Tech. My motto is: "I don't write about things that happen to people, I write about people that things happen to." My website is www.troyduanesmith.com , and my blog is http://tnwordsmith.blogspot.com .

## CHUCK TYRELL

I've read westerns all my life. The first one I remember was Smokey, by Will James. I read everything I could find, living far away from the west in Japan. In 1979, I wrote a western novel for a Louis L'Amour write-alike contest. Didn't win. Decided I could not write fiction. The typewritten manuscript occupied a bottom desk drawer until 2000. I dusted it off and edited it as I input it into a computer file. Sent it off to a publisher, Robert Hale Ltd., in London. They bought it providing I'd cut it down to 40,000 words. The novel is now known as *Vulture Gold*, the first of the Havelock novels.

Besides awards in advertising and article writing, a short story won the 2010 Oaxaca International Literature Competition and my novel *The Snake Den* won the 2011 Global eBook Award for western fiction. Other than that, I just write westerns and fantasy. My home is in Japan, where I live with one wife and one dog and one father-in-law, visited quite often by daughters and grandkids. I write most of my fiction by longhand, usually at Starbucks. Other writing I do on the laptop. My website is www.chucktyrell.com and my blog is www.chucktyrell-outlawjournal.blogspot.com I have a number of short stories lying around in various anthologies.

*Wolf Creek: Hell on the Prairie*

## ACKNOWLEDGEMENTS

"Hell on the Prairie" copyright 2013 by Troy D. Smith
"Drag Rider" copyright 2013 by Charles Whipple
"The Oath" copyright 2013 by Keith Souter
"It Takes a Man" copyright 2013 by Cheryl Pierson
"Asa Pepper's Place" copyright 2013 by Jerry Guin
"Muleskinners: Judge Not" copyright 2013 by Jacquie Rogers
"New Beginnings" copyright 2013 by James J. Griffin

**The Wolf Creek series:**
*Book 1: Bloody Trail*
*Book 2: Kiowa Vengeance*
*Book 3: Dogleg City*
*Book 4: The Taylor County War*
*Book 5: Showdown at Demon's Drop*
*Book 6: Hell on the Prairie*
*Book 7: The Quick and the Dying*

Find them all here!: http://amzn.to/15ez8f6

Also from Western Fictioneers:

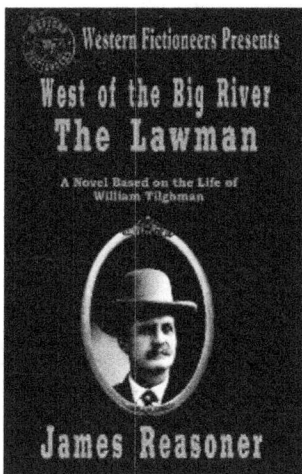

www.westernfictioneers.com

**Western Fictioneers**

Made in the USA
Monee, IL
30 August 2025